New York Times **and** *USA Today* **Bestselling Author**

Lora Leigh

Dragon PRIME

ELLORA'S CAVE
ROMANTICA PUBLISHING

$\mathcal{W}$hat the critics are saying...

∞

Gold Star rating "Ms. Leigh has done it again. She has created a masterpiece that will make you yearn to have a Prime Warrior that will satisfy your heart, body, and soul. With its well-written characters and magnificent plot, <u>Dragon Prime</u> definitely deserves a Gold Star Award. [...] I highly recommend for everyone to run out and to get this novel NOW!" ~ *Just Erotic Romance Reviews*

"First in Lora Leigh's Prime Warrior series, an off shoot of her Legacies series, **Dragon Prime** is an intense beginning. Alyx is a wonderful example of the alpha males that Ms. Leigh is so famous for. [...] I would definitely recommend reading **Dragon Prime**. Be warned that reading the Legacies series to date does help in the understanding of all the "side" players in this story." ~ *A Romance Review*

"Oh my lord this book was good. As I started reading it I thought to myself "Lora's been doing this for a while now [...] let me not be biased on the basis of her previous work" but you know what [...] it didn't matter because this story is a perfect example of why I absolutely love Ms. Leigh's work. Come on how many of us love the whole premise of our man breaking the rules for love? Huh? Cause I love it. [...] The drama and angst are present throughout this story and it creates a world that you really do not want to end." ~ *Fallen Angel Reviews*

An Ellora's Cave Romantica Publication

www.ellorascave.com

Dragon Prime

ISBN 9781419954641

This book printed in the U.S.A. by Jasmine–Jade Enterprises, LLC.

Electronic book Publication January 2004
Trade paperback Publication November 2007

Also by Lora Leigh

๛

About the Author

ജ

Lora Leigh is a wife and mother living in Kentucky. She dreams in bright, vivid images of the characters intent on taking over her writing life, and fights a constant battle to put them on the hard drive of her computer before they can disappear as fast as they appeared.

Lora's family and her writing life co-exist, if not in harmony, in relative peace with each other. An understanding husband is the key to late nights with difficult scenes, and stubborn characters. His insights into human nature, and the workings of the male psyche provide her hours of laughter, and innumerable romantic ideas that she works tirelessly to put into effect.

Lora welcomes comments from readers. You can find her website and email address on her author bio page at www.ellorascave.com.

Tell Us What You Think

We appreciate hearing reader opinions about our books. You can email us at Comments@EllorasCave.com.

DRAGON PRIME

Dedication

෨

Lynn, this one is for you!

*Thank you for the friendship and the support. I hope all
your greatest dreams come true and that your own Prime
Warrior brings you endless nights of satisfaction and
golden days of ecstatic dreams. Good luck in all your
endeavors and may God always bless you and keep you
safe.*

Lora Leigh

Prologue

ॐ

"Alyx. I am dying." Alyx fought within the dream, unwilling to experience the aching regret that filled his soul each time it came to him.

"I cannot save you, Lady Lynn." He brushed her tangled hair back from her face, his heart clenching, the Dragon stone at his chest heating with the sorrow of his clan.

He had fought like a demon to reach the battle, to be by her side, to protect her from the dark forces he knew would go through her to reach the one she protected. She was his warrioress, his bond mate, and he would lose her now, possibly forever.

On his planet his powers would have saved her. He could have drawn on the Dragon stone to heal her, to energize her life force. But this was not his planet. This was an alien world, light years away from his home.

He had no power over such matters on this place called Earth. The Fates and Destiny guiding the souls here had refused him the power to act in their name. Yet, still he had tried. He had fought to make it to her side, to ride the dimensional wave to her rescue. If he could have arrived in time he could have snatched her back. Could have taken her to his home, made her his consort, his heart, as he had longed to do.

He had ignored the directives of the Guardians, had fought the advice of Mother Earth and had done what he had never allowed in all his time as a Dragon Prime. He had given his heart to this woman. No other would possess it now and he had arrived too late to save her.

Blood smeared her gentle face; pain filled her warm brown eyes. She had been her lady's greatest warrior, a protector. Now her lady was dead and soon his gentle Lynn would follow her.

Would they console each other in the afterlife, he wondered. Would they find peace there until their rebirth?

"Will you forget me, Alyx?" Her voice was fainter now, echoing with the terrible pain that consumed her body, the regret that washed through both their souls.

"I will never forget you, little love." He gathered her against his chest, holding her against his heart. "I will await your return, my lady. And I will not let you escape me so easily next time."

He had heeded her wishes to wait before taking her to his bed. Had given in to her pleas that he allow her to fulfill her service to the Mistress of the Wind before giving her life to him. If only he had denied her. If only he had taken her despite her pleas, he could have given her the power to walk away from this battle.

"Alyx?" Her breathing was growing faint now.

He felt tears on his cheeks, amazed that he, such a hardened warrior, could cry. He had seen many deaths, but none had struck at his soul in this manner.

"Yes, my love." He kissed her forehead gently, holding back his scream of rage.

"Alyx, I'm frightened."

His moan was a sob torn from his soul as he rocked her in his arms, his hold on her tightening, his heart breaking.

"Have no fear, beloved," he whispered through his tears. "Only beauty awaits you."

"Don't let me go." He heard her tears then. "Hold me, Alyx. Do not let me…"

"No! No!" His wail shattered the blood-filled valley, his agony resonating throughout the clans, filling the Dragon stone, washing throughout the universe as he laid his head back and screamed out his rage.

"Damn your souls, no!" He came awake, awash in sweat, in memories he could not contain.

His body trembled as his arms clutched at the dream vision that had taken her last breath against his chest. Fought to hold her to his heart, to wipe away the aching, endless loss of his own soul in a bloody, battle-strewn field.

"Lynn." He whispered her name as his fingers clutched the suddenly warming stone at his chest.

It had remained cool all these centuries. He had given his warrior woman his soul. In doing so, he had tied her to the Dragon stone forever, just as he had resigned himself to the endless, aching loss of any comfort he might find in his life of wars and bloodshed.

Yet, the stone had warmed. He lifted it, staring down at it with a desperation that tightened his body to a breaking point. The stone was warm. It was faint, struggling, but it warmed.

"She lives," he whispered in awe. All these centuries he had waited. Had fought another world's battles; had lived with only the periodic comfort of his brothers and his Dragon Master. For this. For this moment. For the assurance that when her soul returned, he would be there to protect her, to shelter her.

"Where are you?" He frowned as he sought the binding. "Show yourself, little one, so I might protect you."

It was not to be. He shook his head, never knowing a time when the stone had failed him, when his powers had not held true.

"You will not interfere." Shock coursed through his body as the form of Mother Earth appeared at the bottom of his bed, taking human shape, her brilliant eyes glowing with power, her expression fierce. "You will not bind her, Dragon Prime, until the time is right. You will not interfere in the completion of the lives of my children. You will search in vain."

He sat up slowly in the bed, feeling his rage build as he faced the woman whom he owed his loyalty to.

"She was given to me!" he raged furiously, his heart clouded by hope and pain. "See the stone..." It glowed clear and iridescent now where before it had been cloudy, gray, sleeping within the mist of incompleteness.

"She was to be given at my leisure," she reminded him coolly. "You interfered, warrior. You will not do so again. Feel her life force. Know she lives and grows in strength. But until her mistress knows the touch of her destiny, you will not know your soul. You will not interfere."

May
Twenty-four years later

Being jerked through the dimensional wave was not Alyx's idea of a fun time. He avoided it all costs. But over two decades of searching had left him desolate, desperate.

After hearing of the report that sped through the warrior clans that the Shadow Warrior had rescued his soul wife, Alyx had known he was a step closer to finding the woman who held his heart. A step closer to vanquishing the danger stalking her at every turn. No longer could he bear the knowledge that her life was in danger and he could not aid her. The Earth Mistress would know her; the Earth stone would hold the answers he sought. He just had to get to her.

He could have waited. He would have waited, but he could sense the growing danger surrounding the woman he could feel on a constant basis, yet could not find. He would not wait again. He would not chance her death this time, as he had so long ago.

The Earth Mistress was as beautiful as she had been a millennia ago. She was wounded, weary, and thankfully sleeping as he approached the bed contained within the primitive aircraft the Earth-based warriors used. Around her neck lay the Earth Crystal, as vibrant and powerful as he had ever known it to be.

He needed only to touch it to know the answers he sought. The woman he searched for was tied to the crystals as well. But this one could give him her location. It could put him a step closer to the woman his soul ached for.

The Mistress's eyes opened then, a shriek echoing around the craft's cabin as she went into warrioress mode. She fought like a man, kicking him away, her fist connecting with his nose and coming to her feet in a single bound. Few men could move so quickly, let alone a female.

Rage filled the room, fear and a determination to survive, but Alyx had no desire to fight this one. For the briefest space in time, his fingers had brushed the powerful stone, though, and he had his answers. That was all that mattered in this moment of time. He knew the woman now. Knew her connection and her face, and from there he could track her.

But the Mistress's abrupt awakening and subsequent scream to alert the warriors required quick action. His fingers touched the Dragon stone at his chest and immediately he was jerked through the dimensional wave to return once again to the house he had taken as his lodging.

His nose bled profusely. Dammit, he hated bleeding. His balls ached. The little witch had slammed her dainty foot directly into them, nearly crushing the three spherical orbs that contained his hope for the future. Why did women always go for the balls? It wasn't as though he tore at their nipples during battle. He was a gentleman, even when delivering the death blow.

Alyx lay face down on the bed now, fighting for breath as the effects of both the blow to his Dragon pride and his equilibrium fought to find balance. One day he would learn to control the wave, he was certain. Not that any of the other Prime Warriors had managed to do so, but Alyx believed in excellence. It was the one area in which he had not achieved perfection. He would conquer it. Eventually. But first, he must conquer the warrioress he had sworn would be his. In every way.

The Dragon stone at his chest heated with the information contained within it now. He could feel her force, could sense her awareness of his sudden connection to her.

He allowed a wicked, purely sensual grin to curl his lips as he turned carefully on his back and stared up at the ceiling of the bedroom. He could feel the shift within her psychic force, the awareness of the sudden bond that had been reestablished. She had escaped him once before. Death had stolen the destiny that was to be hers, for a time. He would not allow such to happen again.

My warrioresses are not so easily conquered, warrior. The voice of Mother Earth struck his brain with painful clarity as he winced at her power.

You should be willing to aid me more, Earth Mother. He felt like snarling. *It is not more than your own soul sister we would save in the completion of this insane game. What should it matter if I gain my soul in return? She is mine!*

The sister of my soul knows no victory is complete or truly won without true defeat of the obstacles in our path. He could sense a most unladylike snort. *Do not come whining to me for an easier way. My daughters suffered death. My sons have suffered a horror unimagined, even to myself, at the hands of your Guardians. Your world is diseased, Dragon. It will take strength and true honor to awaken the sister of my soul. Anything less and she suffers, as do we all. Attain your victory alone, for I will not aid you in this battle.*

And there was the gist of the battle. Earth had become a psychic and oftentimes physical battleground in the war to save the spirit of the planet Alyx called home. Without the females the Prime Warriors were destined to bond with, the evil overtaking their home world would be triumphant. But the Earth Mother refused to allow her children to be taken so easily.

Repayment, Alyx thought. They had brought their evil to this planet and unleashed it on the unknowing life contained on it. For this reason, the bond mates born to the Prime Warriors would not be released until that evil was contained.

It was a highly complicated situation. Guardians and Primes could not kill one another because of the life laws that ruled the two planets. The Guardians had banished Alyx rather than pronouncing death. In doing so, they had punished Earth as well and could do nothing but aid the warriors fighting against it.

The evil was Prime and slowly attaining Guardian power. Jonar, leading the sect of outlaw terrorists known as Blackthorne, was only gaining in power. The forces fighting against the alien castoff had but one last chance to defeat him before he came into a power that this world had no hope of conquering.

The Shadow Warriors and those like them, the strongest of the psychic warriors Mother Earth had created and the Guardians had gifted, now fought the battle against Jonar. To complete that battle, their own bond mates, females gifted with the heart of the Earth's power, had but one more chance to attain the knowledge of their gifts. It was that first one, Chantel Ducaine, the reincarnated bride of the Shadow Warrior, who held the key to the location of Alyx's bond mate.

Those of your world, for all their technology and advancements, are still ignorant of your true place in life, the Mother sneered contemptuously. *You allowed your leaders to steer you from your true course, from the knowledge my sister bequeathed you. Then you whimper and whine when all is nearly lost. Were it not for their own grief should she perish, I would allow your world to become as dust, Alyx. An example to all those who would make such mistakes again.*

Their world was not far from just that. Slowly, the natural order of life was decaying, the breeze growing thin as plant life slowly died in response to the strength that bled from the heart of its power. And she was right. It had been the fault of the Guardians and the Primes, those selected to protect and preserve the land from such evil. The evil had been right under their noses and they had been too foolish, too loyal, to see it.

We will not fail in this. Alyx was determined that no matter the outcome, this time he would not lose the first bond, the woman who held a part of his soul.

We shall see who will win and who will lose. She sounded doubtful of his claim. *But you will not win easily. Nor will you win by want alone. I gave her once into your care and you failed. I will not make this mistake again. This time my daughter is strong, Alyx, well able to defend her own life.*

I aided in her power, he argued furiously. *Her strength comes from my soul.*

Soft laughter echoed around him. *Aye, your power aids her. Your power will give her the strength to either accept or deny your heart. Which, warrior, will she do?*

She was gone as quickly as she had come. Alyx growled in fury at the thought of the fight the woman would most likely hand him now. Mother Earth had given her daughters a stubbornness that would drive even the Dragon Master insane with their rebelliousness.

It would not matter, he assured himself as he allowed his psychic force to center, to calm him and give him direction. She would fight him, no doubt, but he was the Dragon Prime. His skills as a warrior were only surpassed by his skills as a lover, and this time...this time she would be his.

Chapter One
June
St. James Estate
Lexington, Kentucky

∞

Lynn Carstairs tossed restlessly within the light nap she was taking. She could feel him. It was a bond that made her nervous, almost frightened. The invisible path between her force and his had been forged, and she couldn't break it. Hell, break it? She couldn't even make a dent in her need to weaken it.

She had known the connection most of her life. That faint force, that sense of something or someone reaching out to her. But several weeks ago, it had suddenly begun strengthening, as though some cosmic power had shifted, opening the psychic window she had kept firmly locked on the strange being reaching out to her. But now he had her and it seemed to only grow stronger each day. She cursed her powers now more than ever, certain that they were the reason she was being tracked, stalked by the presence.

The psychic powers that had slowly grown over her lifetime had become the bane of her existence, her career, but also her salvation. In the gifts she carried she could lay the blame for her nightmares, her fears and a knowledge she had never wanted. Yet, at the same time, she knew they had saved her life countless times. Hers and her brothers and those she had fought to protect.

Times like this, though, she cursed them more than most. Not sleeping and yet not awake, shifting knowledge moved about her unconsciousness, creating nightmare visions, images of blood and death and monsters too horrifying to remember when she awakened.

She fought each one; terrified it was her own future death coming to her. She didn't want to see it. Didn't want to know it.

She whispered a name then frowned. Whose name did she whisper?

"Where are you?" That question, so often asked of her, was easily enough understood.

"I don't want this," she whispered as she fought to pull away. The force remained strong. "Leave me alone. I'm not who you want me to be."

You were before. You are now. The warrior's woman. Bound heart and soul, mind and body. The dragon arose before her, the air around her becoming heated, sensitizing her body as she gasped in fear. Her nipples peaked. Her thighs clenched as the tender flesh between them began to throb. She saw him, just for a moment; so handsome it was nearly blinding, so wickedly sexual that the sight of him alone was nearly orgasmic. And he brought death...

A strangled cry escaped Lynn's throat as she jerked herself awake, staring around the small sitting room, fighting for breath. For life. Wide-eyed, shaking from the effects of the dream and the sudden knowledge that had tried to overwhelm her, she fought to assure herself she was indeed awake.

She dragged her fingers wearily through her tangled hair as she pushed herself shakily to her feet. It was the stress, she assured herself. The fight to protect Ariel St. James' life was becoming more trying with each attack made against her. Both psychic and physical strikes had been made against the young woman, and despite Lynn's advanced abilities, she felt as though they were slowly losing the battle.

She paced through the rose and cream room, frowning, trying desperately to come up with answers. They couldn't fail. She didn't know why this one mission held such personal importance to her. She couldn't understand the feeling that this job was the most dangerous one she had ever undertaken in her life.

She was jerked rudely from her thoughts at the low ring of the phone on the small table across from her. Striding quickly across the room, she answered it before it could awaken her client, taking a seat on the small brocade chair beside it.

"Hello." It would be one of her brothers, she knew.

"Lynn, I'm sending you reinforcements." Lynn closed her eyes tiredly as her brother's voice seemed to attack her overloaded brain through the receiver of the phone. "Three men are headed in. Dragon, Gryphon, and Phoenix. They'll help hold down the fort until we figure out what the fuck is going on here."

Dragon. She'd dreamed of a dragon. Dreamed of a warrior with wings unfolding as a dragon's cry echoed around her. She fought to assure herself it was coincidence, nothing more. But she couldn't still the sudden sense that her life was getting ready to change irrevocably and that, somehow, this job would change it.

She tried to discount the fear. Tried to push it back where she locked the dreams and images that often tormented her. Dragon. Lynn hoped the code names were a bit more reflective of ability than the last two had been, if nothing else. She had lost three men so far and Blackthorne was getting steadily closer to breaking the shields they had placed around the estate to protect their client.

"I don't like this, Zachary." She held the phone between her ear and shoulder as she glanced back through the open bedroom door to assure herself Ariel St. James was still resting peacefully. "They're breaking even our most advanced security measures. I had two attempts last night and the last one almost made it to the house. We can't afford to lose any more men."

It was the most concentrated attack against any one person that Lynn had seen out of the terrorist group. Silent, deadly, they moved like wraiths through the night and struck with such fatal intent that the battle to hold them back was taxing the entire force of agents Zachary possessed.

Breach Control Inc. was designed specifically to protect against even the most technologically advanced covert terrorist attacks. Armed with the latest in weapons and security gadgets, they had never needed more than a handful of the men and women assigned to a job at a time. Their full force was on this one. Over two dozen of the most experienced, well-trained and psychically aware agents they had on the payroll. Each night, the attacks came closer to the house, and each one was more deadly.

"These three rate off the scales, Lynnie," her brother promised her. "Dragon is the strongest of the three. He was able to put Blaken, Matthew and me in a hold we couldn't even attempt to break, all while he was loading the van with supplies by mental force alone. The other two are nearly as strong. I've never seen anything like it."

Lynn's brow lifted in surprise. Such powers weren't supposed to exist. But then again, the powers Breach Control's agents normally possessed weren't supposed to exist, either.

"What's their ETA?" she finally asked him with a tentative hope that she could catch a few hours of sleep when they did arrive. If they were that strong, then the rest of this assignment should proceed rather easily.

Protect the girl until she healed. That was their job. But Lynn worried. If Ariel St. James was strong enough in full health to protect herself, then how had Blackthorne kidnapped her the first time? Not just that, though. How had they inflicted such damage to her that now, weeks after her rescue, she was still so weak she could barely care for herself?

"Lynn..." A note of warning crept into Zack's voice.

Lynn stilled. She knew her brother. Knew that tone of voice and that it didn't bode well.

"No..." she moaned tiredly. "No bad news, Zack, please. This assignment is going to kill us all at this rate."

A tense silence filled the phone for long seconds.

"Lynn, they're Guardian."

Shock whipped through her body. The Guardians were the worst sort of help. Aliens. A mysterious group of psychic warriors who worked with only select humans in the war against Blackthorne. They were deceptive, powerful, and often too undependable to count on. She did not need this.

She wanted to rap the phone on the antique oak desk and tell her brother just how little she was enjoying herself at the moment.

Guardian. Dammit. Every time she turned around anymore the paranormal aspects of this job were raising their creepy little heads. Aliens. Fucking aliens. Dammit. She didn't need this any more than she needed a resurgence of the nightmares that had haunted her most of her life.

"Lynn, you're not screaming at me." Zack sounded worried. "Listen, these men are good, sis. I promise. They came with Devlin's seal of approval and they're strong. Stronger than anything we've ever seen. And they're willing to help." Which was rare. The question now was *why* were they willing to help? Lynn had her own suspicions where the Prime Warriors were concerned and none of them were comforting.

"Have you ever thought, Zach, that you're not doing anything but dealing with the same things that head Blackthorne?" she snapped. "Every piece of information I have on Jonar leads back to the Guardians. How the hell do we know we can trust any of them?"

Years of working with psychic phenomena as a weapon had taught Lynn to gain as much information as possible concerning those she fought against. The files she had accumulated on Jonar and the select group of Guardian warriors were horrifying. Her first meeting with one of the exceptionally beautiful, powerful beings had been enough for her to know that their powers were too similar to the terrorists of the Blackthorne organization that she had come up against that same year.

"I don't know, Lynnie," he snapped back. "All I know is they are the best I've ever seen or heard. I called Devlin myself and he approved them. He seemed more than relieved they were coming in. That's enough for me."

Devlin was human, but he wasn't normal. Lynn had met him only once and her psychic barometer had gone off the scale the moment he stepped into the room. His power alone was exceptional. And it was his warrior, Shanar the Savage, who claimed Ariel as his woman. Devlin had hired Breach Control to protect her until they could make arrangements to do so themselves. That alone made Lynn suspicious.

If these men her brother was sending her were stronger, then they were in a shit load of trouble if they weren't the good guys. And Lynn couldn't be certain they were the good guys.

"Yeah. Yeah," she sighed as she pushed her fingers restlessly through her short brown hair. Arguing wouldn't help. Her brothers trusted Devlin's word implicitly. "Okay. Devlin trusts them, then we trust them. I know the score, Zack. Who's in charge?"

Her question brought a moment of tense, charged silence.

"Of those three? Dragon is in charge. Of this mission, that hasn't changed. You're in charge, Lynn, and he knows it. He didn't seem to have a problem with it."

Most male psychics of the type Breach Control hired had an instinctive problem taking orders from a woman. The whole alpha deal, she snorted silently. As though because she had breasts she didn't have a brain.

"Fine. When will they arrive?" She began making a mental note of the best place to put them.

"I believe we are already here."

Lynn stilled in shock as the voice, pitched low and filled with amusement and power, whispered from behind her. She turned slowly in her chair, her eyes widening, her chest tightening with some unfathomable emotion that she couldn't put a name to.

"They ride the waves, sis." Zack's voice was little more than a murmur in her ear. "And I'll be damned if they ain't good at it."

The phone clattered to the desk as she rose warily to her feet, staring back at the three huge men. Huge was the only word for it. Six and a half feet tall or better, with wide chests and bulging arms and thighs. They were dressed in black, hair long and flowing, expressions fierce, faces lean and eyes penetrating.

"Fuck!" she wheezed out in shock.

The tallest, his silver eyes glowing, gave her a smile of such sensual threat she felt every nerve ending in her body stand up and scream out in warning.

"Not yet," he murmured, his voice so deep, so powerful, it vibrated through her body. "But soon, Lady Lynn. Very, very soon."

Chapter Two

∞

Okay. They rode the dimensional waves. Lynn was still off balance an hour later as she led the men to the bedrooms she had chosen for them on the upper floor of the house, close to Ariel's. As powerful as she knew they were, she wanted them close by.

The heightened awareness of danger was shifting inside her even before the arrival of the three aliens. Her chest wasn't as tight nor her body as wired with the premonitions of attacks, but her fears for her own emotional and mental safety were rising.

Alyx, Dragon Prime, had claimed her. Standing right there in the sitting room, his silver eyes glowing with promise, he had stated his intentions. As though he had known before arriving that she would be there and that she belonged to him.

She fought to still the trembling in her body, the instinctive urge to flee the house. She could feel him; literally feel his gaze caressing her back, her buttocks and her thighs as she walked ahead of him. Like ghostly fingers caressing her flesh, sneaking between her legs to lick at the sensitized flesh and causing the slick juices there to pool thickly.

It was disconcerting. It made her too aware of her body, too aware of the fact that she had never placed any importance on the fact that she was a woman as well as a psychic warrior. Alyx was making her remember that she was a woman.

"Here's your room." It was at the end of the hall away from Ariel's suite. A large bedroom with dark oak furnishings and a king-sized bed. Big enough for his unusual height with room to play.

Lynn swallowed tightly. She had no intentions of playing with him. God only knew why something so ridiculous had entered her head.

She had intended to stand at the door as he entered but a firm hand at her back had her moving forward in surprise. The door closed behind them, leaving them alone within the dim light of the room.

Heavy shades blocked the sunlight from the large picture window on the far side of the room. The lack of clear light only added to the intimacy that seemed to swirl around them.

"Very nice." He didn't seem to care one way or the other.

Lynn turned slowly, trying to control the hard thump of her heart as she realized he was indeed staring down at her intently, those strange silver eyes seeming to see into her soul.

"I'll let you get settled in then." Why did she keep imagining the dragon of her dreams unfolding around him?

"Lynn." His hand gripped her arm gently when she would have passed, holding her to him as the breath seemed to lock in her throat. "You know me. Do not pretend you don't."

"No," she gasped. "We've never met."

She knew she was deliberately evading the meaning. Unfortunately, she had a terrible feeling she did indeed know him. She fought to remind herself that she did not believe in reincarnation. She did not. She would not.

"Lynn." The soft, unfamiliar accent of his Guardian birth gave his voice a rough, dark sound. "Do not lie to me. I can see the truth in your eyes each time you gather your courage to meet my gaze. Why deny what we both are aware of?"

She was breathing harshly now and couldn't seem to control it. His hand was holding her firmly but she could have easily broken away from him. She wanted to break away from him. Didn't she?

"You're here to do a job, Alyx. Just as I am. Nothing more," she reminded him, though she fought to accept that information herself. "We aren't here to play. And I don't play with Guardians in any way, shape or form. You should remember that."

"There was a time when you were willing to play with me," he whispered.

The vision swamped her. A shaded forest; she was dressed in unfamiliar clothes. Soft tan leather pants, a tunic of sorts. Her hair was long, unbound, flowing in the breeze as the large warrior held her pinned on her back, her wrists shackled by his. She was lifting to him...

"Stop this," she ordered fiercely, jerking away from him and moving several steps into the room to escape the warmth that seemed to emanate from his body and wrap around hers. "I don't like these mind tricks you're trying to play. You're here to do a job, just as I am. Don't turn it into anything more."

"Our jobs are perhaps vastly dissimilar, Lynn," he said quietly, his voice reflective now. "You are here to protect the woman, while I am here merely to claim what is mine. If helping you complete your job paves the way for my goals, then I will do this."

Incredulity seared through her system. "You don't care if she lives or dies, do you?"

He swiped his fingers through the long strands of silver hair. It wasn't the color of middle age, but a rich, vibrant silver, like mercury. Like his eyes.

"I care if she lives or dies, but I cannot make the choice in her life. I will protect her because I am here, and am bound to her life through yours. I am restricted from interfering in human life or death, Lynn. It is for this reason that Prime Warriors do not aid your people as you have continually requested."

"But you are now," she sneered. "How convenient that you can change the rules as you wish."

He sighed in irritation. "I have not changed the rules. You did so when you accepted your destiny in taking this mission. You have come full circle. That circle involves me."

Lynn hid her shock, or so she hoped. She had known from the start that something was different about this job, something different about the friendship that emerged between her and Ariel over the weeks. But this was more than she was willing to accept at the moment.

"Convenient," she said mockingly. "Too bad I'm not fooled so easily, Alyx. I am not unaware of the Prime Warriors, the Guardians or their link to Jonar. I don't trust you or your other alien buddies, so that isn't going to fly with me."

A grin tipped his lips. "I never expected you to do so without a fight," he murmured. "But you will accept the knowledge in time, just as your soul accepted the gifts you now carry during your first life. I have no worries, Lynn. You will accept me now, just as you accepted me before."

There was no amusement in his voice as he finished his declaration. There was rather stone-hard purpose.

"I've had enough of this." She moved to brush past him, to leave the room, to leave the temptation and the questions he represented.

Once again he caught her. He didn't just shackle a wrist, though, he jerked her into his harder, taller body, gripping her hips and lifting her to him as her feet left the ground by several inches.

"Let me go…" She would have torn into him with a furious barrage of orders and insults if his lips hadn't covered hers.

If he had taken the kiss with rough demand, she could have fought him. If he had held her with anything less than tenderness, she would have struggled. She was used to being manhandled. It was required in her training when she pitted herself physically and mentally against her brothers as well as the men she worked with. But she wasn't used to this.

He kept his eyes open, staring down at her with almost drowsy sensuality as his lips rubbed against hers. The friction sent shards of heat piercing her womb, her pussy. It had her gasping, her lips opening, making way for the wicked, gentle stroke of his tongue against the seam of her lips. And still he watched her.

Lynn whimpered, gripping his shoulders for balance, her gaze caught and held by his as powerful, destructive pleasure whipped through her. As though the mere joining of lips had set off a quake of major proportions within her body.

She hadn't come close to finding a way to combat the weakening sensations, when he released her. He lifted his head, those strange eyes glowing with heat, and allowed her to slide down his body. From her thighs to her belly she felt the rock hard impression of his erection burning through her clothes.

"Deny that, little one," he whispered. "If you can."

Chapter Three

ಬ

Not good. Not good. The mantra ran through Lynn's head as she paced the small sitting room outside Ariel St. James' bedroom days later. The soft rose carpeting beneath her feet muffled her steps as she paced back and forth in the room that was twice the size of the largest room she had in her own home.

She could feel the added power of the warriors now prowling the outside grounds. The mental force they fought and lived by seemed to settle over every inch of the estate, snaking into the smallest holes, rooting out the most deceptive traps laid. And there had been several.

Breach Control had known for years that the terrorist network known as Blackthorne wasn't your run-of-the-mill group. No car bombings, no buildings exploding, no loss of mass populations to make a point.

Whatever Jonar was after, it wasn't world domination. At least, not as most groups were after. Jonar was after power. Not monetary power. Not worship. Such men were after a power that was said didn't exist. A power that would leave Earth decimated, broken, unable to support life if it were stolen. Jonar wanted the powerful heart of the Earth, rumored to be under the protection of the Shadow Warriors, Devlin's group of four. Guardian-gifted men who fought against Blackthorne.

Lynn paced to the bedroom door, staring at the woman who still slept peacefully in the king-sized bed of silk and satin. She knew that beneath the linen gown Ariel St. James wore lay the second of four stones that was rumored to be the heart of the Earth. If she died, there would be nothing to stand between Jonar and the theft of it. If she didn't heal, she would never be strong enough to use it to aid in his defeat.

Damn. She remembered a time when she believed such plots, such evil, could only exist in the pages of a book. Psychic power was a charlatan's trick and what little did exist was undependable at best. She had learned differently. Some powers weren't entirely reliable, unless those possessing it learned to control it. Like her. She still had not learned complete control. She could sense evil, could block it, but she couldn't find its source. She didn't have to find its source to fragment its power, though.

The three men who had popped into the sitting room earlier wouldn't have those problems. They were Prime Warriors, Alyx had assured her. The best of the best. Alien. Advanced. Undefeated. She turned away from the bedroom and paced back into the sitting room. She hated aliens. She really did.

"Riding the waves," her brother had called the little trick the three men had used to travel the distance between their offices in New York and the sitting room in Kentucky. A dimensional wave that none of their psychics could reach. They could feel it. They knew it was there. But no one born to Earth had ever learned its use that she knew of.

Dragon, or Alyx, was going to be a problem. She had seen the lust in his eyes, the way he looked at her, as though he were starved and she was the meal awaiting him. Even more confusing was her response to him.

His lips... She drew in a hard breath as her own tingled in remembrance. He had weakened her, made her think of something other than the job at hand or the psychic impressions that often bombarded her brain. His touch had stilled something inside her, had eased the ragged impulses of power that often tormented her. And, she admitted, that scared her more than anything else had in years.

Then there were the psychic sparring matches he seemed to delight in playing with her, waves of sensuality that she fought to block. Sometimes it was no more than the awareness that he was finding a way to catch her alone, to impress upon her the desire that flowed between them. In turn, she was forced to find a way to stay out of reach. At times, it had almost been amusing. At other times, it was too intense for her to bear.

She had taken the coward's way out, though. She had run from him and had escaped him at every opportunity. She was terrified that if given the chance, he would walk away with something she had sworn she didn't possess. Her heart.

The past two days had been harried as the agents attempted to align their powers with the beings suddenly in their midst, so avoiding him hadn't been that hard. It was imperative that they all worked on the same psychic plane. Otherwise, their powers were weakened, diminished, and their abilities to communicate during an attack would be hampered. Learning to work with the Prime Warriors wasn't easy, though.

And though Alyx hadn't overtly stepped in as commander of the mission, the very strength of his power demanded that she stand aside. He knew Jonar and his tactics much better than Lynn or her brothers. He knew how to counter the attacks that Lynn's agents were falling beneath. They couldn't afford to lose more men. But letting go of her position of leadership to the arrogant alien wasn't coming easy. No matter the logic that demanded it, it irked her.

Rationally, she knew it wouldn't have bothered her nearly as bad if it weren't for this reaction she was having to him. She had stepped aside many times for her brothers when their unique strengths outmatched hers in a given area. Several times, she had aided Devlin's warriors, assuming a position of backup rather than leadership in missions that had begun as her own. She felt no resentment when it was required. Felt no need to prove herself stronger than she was. It was seldom necessary.

The very nature of their business demanded that the strongest lead. The one with the most power had a greater ability to stabilize the others and center the force where it was most needed. To do otherwise only endangered the mission and the client.

"You worry too much."

Lynn couldn't halt the squeak of surprise that came from her throat as the alien was suddenly there again. In front of her. Staring down at her with those strange silver eyes.

His long silver hair lay past his shoulders, thick and tempting to touch. If she could reach it, she told herself silently. Every inch of his body was corded with muscle, and between his thighs... She jerked her gaze up, flushing at the knowing glint in his gaze.

"You're supposed to be outside," she snapped, fighting her response to him with every weapon she possessed. "Not in here scaring the hell out of me."

A wicked, knowing glint flared in his eyes. As though he were well aware of the fact that her body liked having him around.

"Hell is a bad place, baby. If you have it in you, then it shouldn't matter how it comes out, as long as it does."

She gaped at him. She would have wondered at his supposed intelligence if his lips hadn't quirked just slightly at the corners.

"Ha ha." She rolled her eyes as she tried to put more distance between them.

She didn't know what that black, form fitting cloth was he wore for clothes, but it made him look too big, too broad, and too damned sexy for her peace of mind.

"You should rest. One of my men will watch the girl." She was sure he wanted it to sound like a suggestion. Unfortunately, it came much too close to an order.

"My post," she snapped. "I'll nap on the couch when I feel all the safeguards are in place."

She couldn't make sense of the psychic waves suddenly surrounding the house. The tentacles of power from the newcomers were too difficult to follow, which made it harder for Lynn to be confident Ms. St. James was safe enough for her to allow herself to rest.

"I give you my word as a Dragon warrior she is safe. Should an attack come, you will be awakened. You need to rest." His voice was infinitely soft, caressing.

Lynn's eyes narrowed as she felt energy weaving around her.

"You put me to sleep and I'll kick your ass on a wave straight out of here," she snarled. "Rein it in, buster. I don't have time for your macho tricks."

The energy dissipated but his amusement seemed to grow.

"Fierce little thing, aren't you?" He glided over to the couch, taking a seat with a casual confidence that smacked of male arrogance.

She wasn't little. She wasn't petite. She wasn't delicate. His tone made her feel like a love kitten and she didn't like it.

"Arrogant bastard, aren't you?" She smiled sweetly.

The wicked smile that tipped his sensual lips had her heart rate picking up in speed. Unfortunately, it also sent her libido into overdrive. She could feel her breasts swelling beneath her sports bra, her nipples peaking. Further down, her pussy was moistening at a frightening rate. She wanted to be fucked. She wanted to be fucked by him, and she wasn't pleased by the thought.

She didn't have time for this. And she sure as hell didn't need to get involved with an alien. God, she needed to be one of the innocent millions who had no idea of the power games being played in the universe.

She was growing tired, she realized with a sense of resignation. Tired of fighting the same battles, the same dark forces, the same nightmares within her own mind. Unfortunately, she was starting to get the feeling that Alyx had more than a little to do with those nightmares.

"Arrogance is worth little without the power to back it up." He shrugged his shoulders casually, the black material rippling over the powerful muscles.

Lynn's fingers curled at the need to touch. Maybe she did need to sleep, she thought with a touch of fear, because she was having a very difficult time keeping her focus here.

She had gone from calm and controlled, to the type of woman she hated above all things. A woman whose body overruled her head. In her entire life she had never been faced with her desires, her needs, overcoming what she knew was best for her and her goals. Learning that Alyx could well become her greatest weakness wasn't a piece of knowledge she welcomed.

"Don't you have work you need to be doing?" she finally sighed as he continued to watch her with those intent, strangely colored eyes.

"I'm going to fuck you, Lynn." He propped his chin on his palm, his elbow braced on the arm of the couch as he watched intently now.

Lynn blinked. He hadn't just said that. Had he?

"Excuse me?" She swallowed tightly. "I don't think I heard you right."

"Yes you did." He smiled with a touch too much confidence. "You just want to pretend you didn't."

She licked her dry lips quickly, fighting back the excitement building through her system and reminding herself, *He's an alien, Lynn. You know. Not human. No red blood. Not Earth-based. Alien.*

"Look, I have a job to do here…" she began furiously, fighting to keep her voice low, to keep from disturbing the woman sleeping in the other room.

"It is being taken care of." He shrugged. "My men are the best, little one. They will let none of Jonar's men through. You may take time to play now."

His eyes seemed to glitter, the strange silvery color deepening, swirling with a sexual threat she had to fight herself to deny.

"Oh, may I?" she sneered as she fought her own response. "Unlike big bad aliens, I like to be certain my job is done and done correctly. So forgive me if I just stumble around on my own here, and do just that. I think it's time you leave."

"Leave?" He lifted a brow with mocking amusement. "I don't think so, my lady. I will not leave you, even for a second. You will not escape me, Lynn. And you will, before much more time has passed, be beneath my body screaming in need for me. I promise you this."

He rose to his feet as she watched him in amazement, astounded by his sheer nerve. She stood stock still as he approached her, certain this had to be some amazing dream that she just hadn't awakened herself from yet. No man, human or alien, could be this arrogant. Could he? Or touch her so deeply in such a short time.

But she admitted that arrogance, that supreme confidence, drew her like a magnet. No man had ever made her want to forget herself, her inhibitions and fears of submitting to such hungers, until Alyx. That he was alien was a problem. But she was starting to fear that it was only a problem because she had unconsciously known that only one of the Guardian warriors could be powerful enough to defeat her. It was hard to desire a man she knew she could best with only the strength of her mind.

The thought that such ability, such power strong enough that it could overcome her own, made her body heat by several uncomfortable degrees.

"Look how hard your little nipples are." Lynn trembled in response as he stepped close to her, his hand reaching out, the tip of one finger touching the hard little point poking through the cloth of her bra and shirt. "I want it in my mouth, Lynn. My tongue swirling around it, making you moan for me. I want this very badly."

She slapped his hand away, jumping back out of reach, her pussy sizzling with a sudden fiery ache to feel him pushing inside her, taking her. Hard. Oh hell.

Lynn put as much distance as she could between her and the strange alien watching her curiously. As though her response was no more than he expected. Her flesh craved his touch. Something hidden in the very core of her being seemed to be awakening, and though it terrified her, she was finding it harder to fight each day.

"Touch me again and I'll leave," she snapped, knowing she couldn't fight herself as well as his touch.

To admit to that weakness was the hardest thing Lynn thought she had ever done in her life. He had a power over her that came close to terrifying her.

"You'll leave?" He tilted his head, watching her with a faintly quizzical look. "Are you not in charge here? I rather expected a threat to force my departure instead."

As though she could force him into anything. She had tried several times already, pitting her power against his and coming out weak and disoriented as he watched her blistering arousal. It had turned him on, sparring with her psychically. It had turned her on as well. And she couldn't seem to manage to turn it back off.

"I'm not a fool." She shook her head as she backed into the desk she had sat at earlier. "You and your men are stronger than my whole force. You don't need us here. You could take care of Jonar yourself."

He shook his head at that. "You are wrong there," he informed her softly. "Her life is tied to your presence. The power you hold is aligned with hers. You will give her strength she will not accept from me. If you leave, little love, she dies. And with her goes the hope of your world. If she dies, then we all fail. Will you risk this?"

She thinned her lips as anger overwhelmed her. He thought he had her, and in a way, he did. But she'd be damned if she made it easy for him. Her body might be caving in to him, but that didn't mean she had to give into it easily.

"Will you?" she retorted softly. "You aren't here out of the kindness of your heart, Dragon. She's important to you as well."

She didn't like the smile that tipped his lips. It was a crooked, amused grin, filled with wicked sexuality and devilish intent.

"Wrong," he whispered. The sound was almost a physical caress. "I come to aid you alone, little love. I come to take what is mine. To claim what was stolen from me before. I came, Lynn, as I have already told you, for you…"

Chapter Four

** спо"**

Lynn was nobody's fool, but she almost believed the declaration Alyx had stated that afternoon. By that evening, she could feel a sense of anticipation, almost a foreboding, trembling in the pit of her stomach as she met him in the deserted living room of the mansion.

She had felt the psychic emanations whispering around the grounds. The threads of power he was laying in place. Even her own people couldn't sense them, let alone penetrate them. But she could. They made her edgy. Nervous. It was a power she couldn't identify or push past and she didn't like it.

"What the hell are you doing?" She stood with her hands on her hips, her eyes narrowing in suspicion at the stone hanging from his neck. It glowed with a rich, mercury as faint wisps of the color seemed to weave about his body and fade into the air around him.

His eyes opened, the tense concentration that had held him coiling in the muscles of his body.

"I'm setting trackers." His voice had roughened measurably, becoming darker, hungrier. "Can you sense them?"

She crossed her arms defensively over her breasts. "Of course I can feel them, and I can't get past them. You're hampering my job, Alyx. Now stop it."

"If you can sense them, then you can weave through them." He began to move about the room, circling her slowly as she watched him with wary interest. "I aligned them with your agents and the powers they possessed to keep from affecting them in the jobs they perform. But it allows me to know each time they reach out, and where the power flows. It eliminates any possibility of betrayal."

His voice was pitched low, the graveled texture of it caressing her senses like rough velvet. She liked it too much.

"My people are completely loyal," she informed him testily. "There's no reason to track them."

"It also tracks any power coming in and where it's headed," he told her. "Jonar's warriors can ride on the power of any of your men and enter the grounds. This is how your men died before."

She had been afraid of that. The two men had been the weakest of the agents, though physically capable of defending anyone. She had sensed something malicious; some tainted feel to their power just before their deaths. She had prayed she was wrong.

"Why can't my people sense the threads then?" He was making her nervous, watching her so closely, gliding with such male grace around her smaller body.

"They aren't powerful enough," he told her almost gently. "I am surprised you sensed them. I thought it would take longer."

He had no more than said the words when she felt a surging force flow from him.

Lynn dropped to the floor and rolled quickly out of the way before coming up with a strong mental shield.

"Good try," she snapped as she felt the force flow back into him.

It had been harmless actually. It would have sizzled over her body, sensitizing flesh sensitive enough already. Sneaky bastard!

"Good catch," he murmured. "What else can you do, I wonder?"

It wasn't a psychic pulse he came at her with; it was physical. His hand stopped inches from her face in what could have been a killing blow. He had managed to penetrate more than a foot of her mental shield before coming to a stop.

Lynn stood perfectly still, staring into his eyes, building on the energy that hummed so strong and deep inside her. As she did, she felt a strange, arousing flare of heat. She could play with Alyx. She could test herself, build her powers and have no fear of harming him. No one, not her brothers nor any of the agents under her, could penetrate her shields in the slightest. But to strengthen them, she had to work them, spar with them. No one was strong enough to allow her the ability to do that.

Alyx's lips quirked as he drew back.

He had exerted very little energy, she knew. If he had wanted to hurt her, he could have. She breathed in deeply, centered herself and flung her senses onto the psychic plane he had established for her and her agents.

"Wimp," he chided her as he moved higher.

She could feel the open gate leading onto the next level. Exhilaration flared inside her. If she could get into that plane then she could learn how to open it herself.

"Where is your power, Lynn?" he called back to her, taunting her. "I dare you to follow me."

She felt the forbidden then. The dark surging tide of unfamiliar energy that twisted in the very bowels of her power's center. The only place she had never delved, had kept locked out of desperation. They were powers she had always known weren't her own. Releasing them, she feared, would release something she had no hope of controlling.

"You want to test yourself, but only on your own terms," he taunted her. "You were given a gift you've denied all your life, and still refuse to see."

He sounded almost angry.

A lifetime of visions stormed through her brain. Visions of blood and death and, as she took her last breath, an alien presence fusing to her soul, traveling with her to wherever she was taken. She shook it off, breathing in deeply. She could reach the next plane without that dark power, she assured herself.

Alyx chuckled as she reached out for the next level. Time and again she pulled on her power, built it, fought to reach him and each time she fell back, defeated.

"You are a frightened child," he told her derisively. "You have the power to achieve your every goal and yet you refuse it. Just as you refused me. Just as you refused life. And now you refuse that part of my soul I bequeathed to you. Perhaps I was wrong to have gifted you after all."

Fury flooded her. She fought the overwhelming wave of weakening emotion. But the damage burned along her nerve endings. She had to control it. What good was the power without the control? She slammed a wave of energy toward his physical body instead, amazed when it connected, almost taking him to his knees.

His eyes glowed. The dragon on his chest seemed to writhe. His eyes lit with a glow of respect.

"You're still cheating," he charged her.

"If you were the enemy, you would be dead," she snapped in return.

"If I were Jonar, you would be in chains, naked and screaming as he fucked your ass to your death, because you refuse to use what was given you."

Dragon Prime

Before she could fight, before she could defend herself, a wave of energy had her pinned to the wall, arms outspread, legs and wrists manacled as she screamed out in anger.

He came behind her, his hand tapping her rear with almost stinging force.

"Jonar likes nice tight human ass," he sneered. "Male or female, makes no difference to him. He's testing not just your men, but you as well. He knows by now that you alone stand between him and Ariel, and he will make you pay for doing so. If he can get his hands on you."

He leaned close as she panted out in fury and fear. "Let me go, Alyx," she demanded roughly.

"Let yourself go," he told her coldly as he moved closer.

Suddenly, the hard ridge of his cock was riding the cleft of her buttocks. "Anal sex is extraordinary," he breathed at her ear. "A blending of power and sensations unlike anything you could know. The complete submission, whether voluntary or by force, of the body you take, be it male or female. Power flows from it unchecked, because it is submission, Lynn. Complete and total submission. The acceptance of the body into that area, opening, gripping; the mind accepts it for what it is. Raping it steals a great surge of mental force from the one being raped. It empowers the enemy. When it is given willingly, the mind opens completely, and power joins. It is greater in this way. But Jonar prefers dark gifts of rage. The force. The pain. The humiliation." He was growing angrier by the second. "And you would give him this? You would take this chance by refusing what you were given?"

"It's not natural," she cried out furiously. "It's dark..."

"It is dark because you deny it." His hands gripped her hips, his cock grinding deeper into her cleft. "Feel me,

47

Lynn. Feel me and know what that bastard will do to you if he gets you. Then say you have reason to deny what I alone gave you." The last was grated out with a voice so filled with anger it shocked her to her core.

He had given her? When? How had he given her such power?

"Figure it out, beloved," he growled. "Because it is your only chance at survival, as well as Ariel's. And I suggest you figure it out quickly."

He stepped away from her, the power holding her releasing her as suddenly as it had captured her. She turned, breathing hard, staring back at him in shock.

"What is it?" she demanded. "That power? You know what it is."

"As do you." His eyes were almost frightening to see now, they glowed so richly. "As does your body."

She realized the changes then. Her breasts were swollen and hot, her nipples so hard that her deep breaths were rasping them against her bra, sending hard electric shocks straight to her overheated pussy.

Her eyes widened in alarm.

"When you open yourself to that power, Lynn, then you will know the answers you need. Until then, you are a danger to yourself and anyone you work with. Because Jonar knows you now. This mission, your interference with his designs for Ms. St. James, assured it. He will take you. He will steal that power and laugh at you for your weakness. If there is anything Jonar loves more than terror, it is the moment his victims realize exactly what he had stolen from them. With you he will take more than your power, he will steal a part of mine as well. So not only do you die, beloved, but a part of me dies with you. Because you were too stubborn to fucking care." He grew angrier with each word until the final phrase was growled out so harshly she flinched painfully at the emotion behind it.

"No." She shook her head, feeling knowledge swirling in the air around her. She couldn't accept it. She *wouldn't* accept it. "I don't like your games, Alyx. And I'm starting to not like you."

She didn't give him the chance to answer. Didn't give him the opening to charge her further. She swept quickly from the room and moved at a fast pace back up the stairs, back to the safety of Ariel's room. But no matter how far or how hard she ran, she had a feeling she would never escape the door Alyx had opened, whether intentionally or unintentionally, into that dark power.

She could feel it growing stronger now, unwilling to sleep as it had for years. Just as he had awakened her body, and her once slumbering desires.

Chapter Five

ഇ

"The Mother has forbidden it," Lynn whispered desperately as Alyx's kisses filled her with a need that rocked her to her soul. "I swore my life to Ariel. I cannot betray her and the gifts given to protect her, Alyx."

She was desperate for his touch, though. Desperate for the hot kisses, the gentle hands. But she had been warned. The loss of her virginity meant a loss of her powers. She could not take this chance.

"I can replace anything you might lose," he vowed hungrily. "I swear it, beloved. Your innocence will but give us both greater strength. I swear this to you."

His body was hard, heated, his bare chest burning against her linen-covered breasts as he moved against her.

"Not yet," she gasped as his lips feathered against hers. "Let me see her through this one last test. Shanar takes her soon to his homeland. Once they are on the ship that will carry them away, I will relent. I swear it, Alyx. Let me be certain."

It was only a fortnight away. Her Mistress and the man she had wed would depart the dark atmosphere of the castle then and attempt to find solace in a new life. The death of Ariel's sister had nearly destroyed not just her, but everyone who had lived within the stone fortress the sorcerer had built for his daughters. The magic the sorcerer had wrapped about the land ensured that the death was forgotten within the minds of those who loved Chantel the greatest. But within the hearts, the woman lived on.

Lynn had barely known Chantel. The magic had not reached her as it had the others. And the night the spell had been cast Alyx lay with her in her bed, a shield of his power enfolding them.

Nothing could touch her there. Nothing could touch her as long as she lay within his arms.

Alyx groaned. "A fortnight," he whispered. "I can bear this if I must. But if I cannot have your body, at least allow me your heart, Lynn. Give me that gift alone to sustain me."

She stared up at him, breathing heavily. She knew what he asked. If she allowed him to breach that barrier then they would never be apart, not even in death. He had explained this to her. That the power he held would fuse with her soul, marking her for eternity as his heart.

She had accepted him as her soul.

She relaxed against him, her eyes closing, her arms falling to the bed beneath her as she felt him groan in pleasure. Their bodies couldn't mate, not yet, but their souls could.

It was unlike anything she could have imagined, feeling his power touch hers, penetrate it, fill it until pleasure was like a cascade of exploding flames within her mind. In that instant they were joined forever. A part of each other.

Then the dream shifted. Instead of hazy, floating pleasure, it became an agonizing pain, a sense of hopelessness and futile regret.

"Take the power, beloved," Alyx's voice was grief stricken within her vision. "Take it, for both of us. I will wait forever if I know there is but a chance."

His power weaved about her soul, seeking to merge with it again as it began to lift free of her lifeless body. She was dead. She knew she had died there within his arms.

"For me, beloved." Tears fell on her white cheeks as the soft fog flowed from the Dragon stone at his breast. "For me. Allow me this chance to know you but once more."

What he was giving her was a piece of all he was. Not just his soul, but the very heart of his peace, his contentment, a part of the phantom that had followed him for so very long. A part of the power forged with his own blood and carrying a part of all he was.

Her heart opened, her soul eased, and she felt that part of him flow into her, warm her as she entered the cold, hallowed halls of death…

Lynn came awake gasping, her body damp with sweat, fear racing through her, pumping in her breast. The mists of her dreams were lightening as they never had before, showing her glimpses of things she neither wanted nor asked for.

She breathed in deeply, containing the gasps that would have shuddered from her body. Alyx. Alyx was the man who had haunted her dreams for so many years. It was his power that had flowed into her on her death, not some evil force as she had always feared. It was he.

Her hands covered her face as that realization rocked her soul. She did not believe in reincarnation, she assured herself. She was not some damned warrior woman reborn. She was just Lynn Carstairs. That was all. A woman with too much power and too many fears.

But she knew there was more. Denying it wouldn't make it go away. And she knew the man who had the answers she needed.

* * * * *

Could he wait much longer? Alyx lay in the bed of the room Lynn had assigned him, naked, aroused. Without the protection of his skin cloth, the sensitive flesh of his body began to absorb the psychic resonations of the woman bound to him.

The black skin cloth was all that often protected a Prime Warrior from a nearly uncontrolled lust before he convinced his bond mate to come to him. The psychic energy was often a double-edged sword. He could feel her arousal, her need, stroking along his skin like a Dar-phantom's touch. The misty wraiths of his home world were pure sexual energy, bequeathed to a warrior when his bond mate accepted him.

The Dar-phantom was pure pleasure, to both the male and the female who shared a Dragon stone, as he and Lynn did. A shudder of pure lust shook his body at the thought of the creatures, of watching his beloved Lynn being prepared for her own Dragon stone.

His cock flexed in hunger, the silky pre-seminal fluid seeping from the dual openings at the tip of his cock as his balls tightened in need. He glanced down the line of his body, seeing the organ stretching up his abdomen, so different from a human male's cock, both in looks and in function.

The thick male flesh was heavily veined, the wide ropey ridges nearly as sensitive as the cock's crest beneath the head. Prime Warriors alone possessed the firm extension below the crown of their cocks. It was an indication of their power, both in strength and in sexuality. During the sex act, the firm, flexible ridge absorbed psychic power, stroked and caressed, as their cocks would thrust inside a tight pussy.

And it would be tight. So exquisitely tight that the seminal fluid that flowed from the two small openings on the head of his cock would be needed to help relax the snug little channel.

He groaned at the thought of it. His beloved was so delicate, so dainty, that the thought of fucking her had his cock pulsing in need. So much need that he knew he could not survive seeing her again without relief.

One hand moved over his chest, his fingers tugging the solid gold loop that pierced his left nipple. The other moved down to his straining erection, gripping it, spreading the natural lubrication over the sensitive shaft as he imagined pushing into the snug cunt between Lynn's firm thighs.

He groaned. As tight as her pussy would be, the delicate tissue of her anal channel would be even more so. When they were bonded and the Dar-phantom was called to create her Dragon stone, then he would know that sweet entrance as well.

His hand tightened on his cock as he stroked slowly over the shaft, squeezing it, mimicking the tight grip he knew he would find when he finally filled Lynn's sweet pussy.

He would fuck her slow and easy at first. Work his cock into her sheath as she trembled and shook beneath him, her pussy convulsing as it strained to take him.

Alyx shuddered at the thought as he stroked his cock, his hips and thighs tightening at the tension filling his body. She would scream for him, he thought, as he separated her cunt muscles, stretching them with a pleasure that would ride that fine, agonizing line of pain that a warrior sought to give his bond mate.

She was a virgin. Not so much innocent as she was untried. And, oh, how he wished to try her. His cock plunged forcibly through the grip of his fingers as his hips jerked in response to that thought. He would open her slowly, his cock penetrating, stretching her until he came to the thin veil of her virginity. There he would pause. His hand stilled. He would stare into her eyes, watching the dark depths, feeling her strain beneath his body as his cock leaked the seminal fluid that made all sexual acts more pleasurable for their females.

It would loosen the obstruction, allowing him to stretch her slowly, to slide inside her as she cried out in pleasure. She would be tight and hot. Her heat would surround his cock as it conformed to each ridge, gripping it like a glove that had become a shade too small.

His hand tightened. He moaned as he began to stroke the flesh harder, picking up speed as he imagined her beneath him, her legs splayed wide as he watched her take him. Watched his flesh impale her, fuck her with all the pent up lust that had only built over the human centuries.

She would be so slick with the combination of her lubrication as well as his own. The sound of the moist thrusts would fill his senses; the sight of her cream soaking his cock would make him insane to fill her with his seed. He would hold her thighs wide open, watch as his hips picked up the pace, burying his aching dick inside her pussy until she began to convulse around him. Until she shuddered, screamed, and he felt her orgasm flowing along the tightening veins that carried his seed when he exploded.

It would trigger his own climax. He would bury himself deep and hard inside her, allowing his control to falter, to release the load tightening at the base of his cock. His orgasm would send shafts of lightning-hot energy flowing through his body, infusing his seed, blasting into the exquisite grip of her pussy and pushing her into an orgasm that would bind her sexuality to his forever.

Their energy, psychic and physical, would merge and the first ritual of the bond mate would be completed. The thought of it had his teeth gritting, his hand moving faster on his straining erection. His body tightened. His scrotum began to vibrate. A second later his release surged through the thick shaft as a muted groan escaped his chest.

Silky, hot seed shot from his cock, splattering along his abdomen to his chest in two strong streams of his fertile come. He fought for breath as energy surged through his body, searching for an outlet and finding none. His hips jerked in reaction as a last pulse of semen spilled from the tormented flesh.

"Oh. My. God!" Horror filled the female voice that echoed from the connecting doorway.

Dragon's eyes snapped open. Lynn's face was pale, her eyes wide in disbelief, her lips parted as she stared at his still-hard organ. Breathing in roughly and fighting for control he leaned up on his elbow, looked from his cock to her shocked face, and chuckled in delight.

"Don't worry, darling," he drawled. "The monster doesn't bite. At least not yet."

Chapter Six

ഇ

Don't worry darling, the monster doesn't bite... Lynn stood outside the St. James mansion the next morning, enjoying the heat of the sun, fighting to ground herself back in reality, rather than the events of the night before. The dreams were bad enough. But what she had seen moments later had shocked her to her core.

Or was it really a nightmare? She wiped her hands over her face as she stared around the pristine grounds, seeing the evergreen shrubs, the borders of blooming perennials, the elm and maple trees that shaded the two-story white brick mansion.

She hadn't slept. She had been too terrified to close her eyes, to take her gaze off the locked door that separated her room from Dragon's. Afraid the dreams would return. Afraid he would enter. And if he did, she didn't know if she could deny him. Not when everything inside her yearned for him.

He wasn't human, she reminded herself. She had known that. She didn't know why she expected him to look human...*there.*

She pushed her fringed bangs back from her forehead, convincing herself that the moisture on her forehead and over her lip was due to the heat. It had nothing to do with the memory of seeing Dragon jacking off the night before. What he had been jacking off was what threw her off balance.

The monster doesn't bite... She bet that was the only thing it didn't do. It was thick and long, heavily veined, though appearing ridged, and beneath the head—she shivered in what she convinced herself was fear—it was much thicker, appearing rather like a rooster's comb running down beneath the thick tip of the erection. It was a dark as the rest of his body and heavily bronzed.

She swallowed back her whimper as she felt her cunt ripple. Fear, she told herself. She was frightened, not aroused. And the *monster,* as he called it, was something to be frightened of.

But was it really fear? That was the question that tormented her. Fear wouldn't leave her weak and wet. It wouldn't make her hunger to run her lips and tongue over the unusual cock. It wouldn't make her mind fill with images of Alyx taking her, dominating, stealing her will and replacing it with his own, a will to spread her thighs and open herself to him. To feel the monster impaling her with hard, strong thrusts. No, that wasn't fear.

She grimaced as she realized what it was, realized that some of the nightmares of her past had been but misty warnings of what was coming. Her body supine, defenseless and vulnerable as she screamed. She had thought in pain, in fear. But as she shifted through the dark dreams she realized something more. It wasn't pain. Wasn't fear. Rather it was pleasure, exacting and brutal in its intensity, and she was beginning to crave it.

This mission was the most important one of her life and Lynn knew it. Ariel St. James had to live. She had to regain her strength to use the power embedded within that crystal. But even more than that, Lynn had known her place was by the other woman's side, her power bracing the other woman's until she could regain her strength. Just as she was beginning to realize that Alyx was a part of that power and her mission here as well.

"Lynn, pull your men in closer to the house." Dragon's voice filled the comm. link at her ear as her body suddenly went on alert.

"Pull in." She sent the order out quickly as she turned and raced back into the house. "Assume base position."

The order would have the two-dozen men and women surrounding the house. Half inside, half out.

"What's going on?" She couldn't sense the psychic waves of malice that usually accompanied a strike. "They've never attacked in daylight before."

She sprinted up the curved staircase to Ariel's room.

"They're moving in a more conventional pattern now," Alyx said softly as she slid silently into the bedroom and positioned herself beside the bed. "You have two four-men teams moving along the mountain in assassin formation. Keep your men alert, but I don't think we'll have a problem."

Ariel was sleeping comfortably, a light flush of health on her cheeks as her body healed. Lynn quickly checked the bulletproof shutters that had been installed on the windows and the position of the bed away from them.

"Dragon, you keep me up-to-date," she murmured quietly, unwilling to awaken her client.

The aliens communicated telepathically, a power she didn't possess herself. Very few of her people did, so it wasn't a dependable means of communication until Lynn and her warriors learned how to break through that final barrier on the psychic plane Alyx and his men had guided them into.

"Always, my love." She winced at the shocked gasps and strangled snorts from the two-dozen men and women who worked under her.

She didn't dignify the statement with an answer.

"Liz, you and Jack get up here with me," she ordered two of the strongest psychics on the force. "If it's Blackthorne men, I want a ready source of power."

Providing the psychic shield needed to keep the terrorists from invading the room with their own waves of power had been steadily draining her strength. She hated using anyone else because of the danger involved, but she was too frightened that her own energy would fail when they needed it most.

"I will be there to aid you should you need it, Lynn," Alyx countered the order. "I merely need your people out of harm's way. Sometimes Jonar gets brave and sends his own force as a last resort. Your people cannot come against them."

The calm strength in his voice seemed to aid her failing powers. She took a deep breath and fought to relax as Liz and Jack entered the room. They took their positions. Those two on one side of the bed, Lynn across from them.

"Lynn, do not attempt to shield her yourself." Dragon's voice was firm now. "It will drain you too much. I promise, we have this under control."

"You do your job, big boy, I'll do mine," she said quietly as she nodded at the other two agents. They would support her if her strength failed. She had never failed before.

"Lynn." Dragon's voice hardened as she relaxed back in her chair, closing her eyes and taking a deep, fortifying breath.

She ignored him. She cleared her mind as she allowed the power that seemed to hum in the very center of her soul to gather. It began to build, to gain in strength as she opened herself, directed the energy and let it free.

Lynn didn't open her eyes, but she knew what the other two agents saw. The thin, misty-like dome that surrounded Ariel would be impenetrable by all but the strongest psychics. If needed, Lynn could call on the power of her entire force to lend their strength.

She could hear Dragon cursing. The sudden freedom, the opening of her senses, allowed her to see so much more as well. The assassins heading in weren't mere psychics. They were warriors, much as Dragon and his men were, but hopefully not as strong.

The immortals. As always she had to fight her terror when knowing they were near. They were without souls, without mercy, and their power was so strong that even she had not sensed the dark cloud of energy pouring in front of them, ready to strike at the weakened Ariel at the first opportunity. But she saw more as well; a golden wave of energy meeting the dark cloud, directed by Dragon and his men.

Before her amazed senses she saw a battle waged on the psychic plane that she knew she might never glimpse again. Golden streams of power arched into the metaphysical level, meeting the dark menacing cloud head on. Flaring energy erupted in waves as each attack directed toward Ariel was thwarted before ever coming close to the dome Lynn had placed around her.

Snaking bolts of lightning, fire and pure electricity tore through the ominous power Blackthorne's men had placed before them. On the ground, gunfire began to erupt as the terrorists shot wildly, desperate to wound or kill whoever dared to meet them with such strength.

The entire battle played before her mind as Dragon's force played almost lazily with the enemy. She could see him, as plain as she would have if her eyes were open and she was standing beside him. He was sharpening the blade of a sword. A sword, for God's sake. No conventional weapon. He showed no sign of stress or concern. Playing with the enemy as he tore a path of careless destruction through their psychic force.

Chapter Seven

ന

Within minutes it was over. The dark gray cloud slowly cleared, leaving four immortals slowly disintegrating to dust on the forest floor. Lynn collapsed as she pulled the shield back, allowing the power to flow back into her weary body. She didn't open her eyes, even though she heard Liz's gasp. She knew who was there.

The long, silken strands of his hair flowed down her back as he bent to pick her up. She felt it, like a caress, over the skin of her shoulders and back. Lynn felt her nipples peak, her pussy clench in hunger. She was weary, weak, and craving his touch as she had never hungered for anything in her life. It terrified her.

"Keep the monster reined," she ordered him weakly as he lifted her quickly from the chair with a sharp command to the other two to stay with Ariel.

He strode from the bedroom, his steps quick as he moved through the house.

"I should spank you," he snapped as he kicked a door closed behind him. "That was a foolish thing to do, Lynn. Did you not trust me to do as I said I could? And barring that, could you not at least have harnessed your true power? For pity's sake, woman, you will be the death of yourself."

She grunted as she bounced on a bed. His or hers? She opened her eyes wearily, relieved to see it was her room, her bed.

"As though you would be of any use to me sexually in this shape," he snorted, waving his hand over her body.

"Dragon." She jerked the comforter over her suddenly nude body. Her clothing lay on the floor as though it had never covered her flesh.

"Look at you." The restrained violence in his voice as he suddenly covered her body with his own caused her to tremble in reaction.

Lynn stared up at him, fear and lust snaking through her system as the heat of his body seeped through the blanket and sank into her flesh. Her legs were held tight between his, his chest pressing against her abdomen, her wrists shackled to the bed by his hands.

"Do you think that covering hides you from me?" he snarled furiously. "Shall I show you how easily I can dispose of it?"

Just that quick it was gone, fluttered to the floor as she watched with wide, amazed eyes.

"I am like nothing you have ever known." He bared his teeth at her, his silver eyes darkening, swirling with flashes of electric fury. "You do not disobey me. You do not place your body nor your mind in danger…"

"Don't tell me what to do." Lynn struggled against him weakly, unwilling to lie still, to be helpless beneath the shards of pleasure tearing through her body.

He was only lying against her, she groaned silently. Yet her body was soaking his weight up, trembling in fascinated ecstasy at the feel of the heat pouring from him. Her pussy was on fire. She couldn't believe it. She had never felt so empty, so needy for something to fill that hidden channel in all of her adult life.

And her breasts. His eyes were trained there, watching her nipples harden, her breasts swelling as his gaze seemed to darken.

"I'm going to fuck you until you can do nothing but lie beneath me and whimper with each orgasm ripping through your body," he growled. "When you are too weak to move, too weak to even cry out as my cock is surging hard and deep inside your pussy, I'm going to give you every drop of come building in my balls. And trust me, baby, I have quite a load stored up for you. Then perhaps you will be willing to accept all of what I have given you, Lynn. All of it."

Her eyes widened in shock as she began to shake her head almost violently. Unfortunately, she couldn't seem to remember how to say no.

"You will sleep first." He seemed to only grow angrier as he watched her. "Your face is gray, Lynn. You cannot even gather the energy to struggle against me because you refuse to allow yourself that freedom. When I fuck you, you'll at least be awake enough to keep your damned eyes opened."

"You're insane," she gasped, her body burning for him now despite her unwillingness to allow that monster rising between his thighs into her cunt. No way. No how. Her cunt was singing a different tune, unfortunately. "You are not fucking me with that, that *thing* you have for a cock."

His eyes narrowed, the planes of his face tightening with anger.

"Thing?" Silky menace filled his deep, resonating voice. "That thing? Oh, darling, when I shove that *thing* up your tight little pussy you'll be screaming a different story then, I promise you that."

Her body already was. His breath washed over the tip of her full breast, creating a streak of lightning-hot pleasure that struck her pussy like an arrow of lust. Her clit was straining between the bare folds, throbbing and swollen as the juices spilled from her vagina, pooling between her thighs. Energy hummed within her weary body, but it wasn't the pure natural energy of her own power. It was that dark center raging, straining for release.

"Ah yes." He moved against her, his gaze centering on the hard nipple. "You know, don't you, beloved, that denying me won't last forever."

Her fingers curled against her palms as she felt him shift his weight, pressing between her thighs, settling his hard abdomen against the slick, moist mound of her sex.

Lynn whimpered as the material of his clothing brushed against her straining clit.

"Stop," she finally gasped as he ground against the sensitive little nub.

"Stop?" he whispered. "I can still the fires, Lynn. I can please your body without taking you as I want to. I can make you sleep relaxed and dreamless, your body replete."

As he had in her dreams. Their souls merging, a mating dance filled with more pleasure than she could ever imagine.

Lynn couldn't stop the moan that tore from her throat. "This is insane. It won't work. You're not even human," she wailed desperately.

His hands lifted from her wrists. Lynn moved to push away from him, only to find that even though he had released his grip, she was still shackled to the bed. She stared up at him in surprise.

"Humanity does not begin and end on this planet," he growled as her thighs were spread apart by unseen hands, her hips lifted, opening her to him, baring the smooth flesh of her cunt for his inspection. "You can say no, Lynn. At any time."

Could she? She was watching his face instead, seeing the hunger that transformed it, that lit his eyes with carnal intent and gave his expression a wicked, sinful cast. Then he licked his lips.

"If I dare to lower my lips to such perfection, I may not rise from the banquet until we both collapse from exhaustion," he said regretfully. "But I will not leave you to ache this way, little love."

She felt the plump swollen lips of her pussy spread.

"Dragon." He wasn't touching her in any way.

"Your perfect little clitoris is swollen," he whispered. She imagined she felt his breath against the overly sensitive bud as she panted for breath. "Your sweet nectar lies thick and glistening on the curves of your cunt, tempting me to taste."

Her breasts were heaving as she fought for air. Lynn was certain she was going to pass out any minute from the sheer excitement of the moment.

"Come for me, little one," he whispered then, his voice deepening as he stared into her eyes.

He wasn't touching her, Lynn screamed out in shock to her inner self. Not touching her. But she felt his mouth anyway, it surrounded her clit as the sensation of a tongue rasping, licking, a mouth suckling, drawing on the little bundle of nerves. It took only seconds. Her body was primed, aroused, lust whipping through her system like a wildfire, consuming her.

Something in her mind shifted, opened. In that moment she felt him flowing into her, felt pleasure whipping through her body, her mind, stopping only at the shield she had placed around that dark center of her soul.

She exploded in a blaze of heat and light so intense she feared she would never survive it. It rocked through her body, rasping each nerve ending, sending waves of pleasure so intense, so astounding, pouring through her system that she screamed out at the rocketing release.

"I have lost my mind," she heard Dragon growl as he threw himself from the bed, releasing her as the blanket was thrown over her once again. "Look what you have done to me. You have made me an insane man. Damn you, when will you stop this senseless fear of me?"

Lynn opened her eyes despite the drowsiness tugging at them. He gestured to his body, the thick ridge of his cock rising along his lower stomach, covered only by the snug material of his clothing.

"Hmm," she murmured, remembering well the sight of it, frightened to realize just how badly she did need to fuck him.

"I should not be like this." He frowned at her heavily, a male pout crossing his expression. "I should be buried inside you, finding my release with you, not playing these childish human games of touchy-feely. It is insanity."

Her body still hummed with need, but her mind was slowly shutting down. Exhaustion washed over her, bringing with it a veil of complete and utter darkness.

* * * * *

Alyx stared at Lynn as she slipped into sleep. Her expression smoothed, the fear and the lust leaving it, settling into lines of weariness as her body relaxed. He sighed in frustration. Soon, he promised himself as he touched the heated medallion at his chest. It was a dragon surrounding the iridescent silver of the stone.

The stone was the heart of his planet, of the powers that had been given to him upon his completion of his warrior's quest. It was his protection, his solace while away from his home world. In it, he carried all the things needed to complete him should he find his bond mate on a world other than his own. The final ritual of his bonding with Lynn would release the Dar-phantom, who had made this journey with him, and the other medallion that would complete the binding of their hearts and of their souls.

But, the journey ahead would not be easy. She fought him. She denied him her body, even though she could not whisper the words denying his touch. Her mind would not accept. Until she accepted the need she had for him, he could not take her. Until her heart accepted her feelings for him, the Dar-phantom would not come forth. The ritual of the mating could not be made without her full cooperation and desire. He sighed heavily. This might well be the hardest battle of his life.

Chapter Eight

∞

"You stay away from me." A slender, trembling finger poked into Alyx's chest as he stepped into the kitchen the next morning, praying for coffee. It was his one true weakness, the taste he had developed for the dark, bitter brew.

But rather than a cup of steaming energy, he was instead greeted by a more than irate little vision of simmering lust and fury. He lifted a brow in surprise as he looked down at the small digit digging into his breastbone.

"A bit to the left," he murmured. "It would do much more damage over the piercing there."

Her eyes narrowed at the challenge before she sniffed in disdain. The sharp, nailed little weapon retreated as she turned her back on him and paced over to the counter. His gaze followed her then became distracted by the steaming pot beside her. He rubbed his hands in glee as he directed a ceramic mug from the shelf, and the coffee pot from its base.

Lynn turned back to him, crossing her arms beneath her breasts as she watched the psychic manipulation. He paced over to the pouring coffee, gripping it in his hands as he mentally returned the pot to its resting place. He smiled over at her with something he hoped wasn't complete anticipation. He could feel her body throbbing, the heat reaching out to him. She would not be able to deny him much longer.

"It was a calm night last night," he said as he took his coffee to the long table sitting in front of a large paned window.

Sunlight poured through sunny yellow curtains, warming the wood bench table and sparkling on the pristine white appliances and adobe tile floor. It was a nice, spacious room. Clean and smelling nicely of spices and herbs. It was homey, which he hadn't really expected. Most influential humans that he knew rarely stepped into their kitchens unless forced to do so. It was the domain of the staff only.

"Breakfast was hours ago," she informed him, ignoring his comment. "You missed out."

He shrugged his shoulders. "I ate with my men earlier this morning. There were details to iron out."

"Details?" she questioned him with false patience. "I would hope you are not planning *details* on my mission without informing me?"

"Actually, perhaps I was." He smiled over the rim of his cup before sipping at the tempting drink. Ahh, yes. He could almost feel the caffeine soaking into his pores, the flavor nearly a carnal delight as it washed over his taste buds.

"Dragon, this isn't going to work." He stilled as her expression turned resolute. "This is my job, my responsibility. Just because your powers are stronger than mine doesn't make you boss here."

He leaned back in his chair, taking another, longer sip of the coffee as he watched her.

I could teach you the power. He allowed his mind to touch hers, his thoughts to flow through her.

A strong mental shield immediately snapped into place as her face paled.

71

Really, beloved, as though such a shield could keep me from your mind. Or your body. He smiled, swallowing his coffee with a murmur of appreciation.

"Stay out of my head, you alien pervert." Her eyes flashed dark fire, her cheeks flushing with anger as he glimpsed her sudden memory of him pleasuring himself.

Alien pervert? He took another deep drink of the coffee. He would need patience for this woman. She had not been nearly so stubborn in her past life.

"So help me, Dragon, if you don't stop this insanity I'll shoot you myself." She pushed her fingers through her hair in a gesture of frustrated fury.

Her hair was too short. He didn't like it, he thought as he watched her. Before, it had been long and flowing when freed from her braid, falling to her hips and creating a cloak of fragrant silk down her back.

It was now cut above her shoulders, tapering back from her face, and though it gave her face a pixyish look, and was still more than attractive, he couldn't forget the need he had once had to have all that hair brushing over his body. His eyes narrowed on her head for a second.

He watched as she frowned and ran her fingers through it again, massaging her scalp. Ah, some things must just be done an inch at a time, he thought in satisfaction. Growing hair, fucking into a tight sheath, there were times when patience was needed. Yes, the added inch of soft silk looked much better.

"So, you are threatening to shoot me now," he sighed as though saddened. "It is a cold, cruel world when a man cannot even show his desire and his need for his chosen woman. I believe my heart may be breaking."

"Not," she snorted as she flashed him a disdainful look.

She was once again dressed in one of those snug little tank tops, a forest green this time. He would like to see her in black skin cloth, the material shaping over her breasts rather than confining them as the snug bra beneath her shirt did now. Skin cloth would hug and love her body, bring her pleasure, keep her cool when needed, warm when the temperature dropped.

He rubbed a hand over his chest at the thought. Yes, a gift of skin cloth would be a good idea.

"What are you up to now? This habit of yours of trying to run my life is going to piss me off," she informed him as she propped her hands on her jeans-clad hips. Skin cloth for certain. Shirt, pants and soft-soled shoes. Those jeans would be rough against his flesh and would take more energy to remove than it took for his cock to part the cloth that was part of his home world.

His body clenched at the thought. He could merely lift her against him and the material would part for the heavy length of his erection. He would move between her thighs as her cloth parted at the tiny slit of her entrance. He almost groaned at the thought. There was nothing like fucking as the cloth caressed your body. It was almost as good as fucking nude.

Of course, after the first wearing of it, her body would develop the ultra sensitivity that came from its use.

"You're scary," Lynn said softly as she watched him.

He raised his eyes from her soft curvy hips and met her gaze.

"How so?" he asked her, braving the heat of the coffee for a longer drink.

"If you could see your face you would know," she grunted as she moved to the coffee cup she must have set down earlier.

He watched as she refilled it, admiring the curves of her rear, imagining his hands parting them, his fingers finding the small little rosette of her anal entrance, stroking it, opening it...

She turned around slowly. He gave her an all too innocent look and sipped at his coffee again.

"Ms. St. James is sleeping well this morning then?" he asked her, as though he hadn't been imagining fucking her tight little ass.

She rubbed a hand over the curve of her ass as though confused by some sensation there and nodded slowly. "She was awake for a while this morning. We have to keep the shields carefully in place while she's awake. Her control is so shaky right now it would be easy for one of Jonar's men to latch onto it and slip past us undetected."

That was a problem. Psychic waves were damned hard to control unless they were your own. Ariel was still so weak, physically and emotionally, from her ordeal that her natural controls were still shaky at best. In most cases, psychics protected themselves from others detecting and riding into their unconsciousness on the waves of their power. The mind would automatically block even one of Dragon's powers from doing such a thing. But in Ariel St. James' case, her mind was fighting so hard to repair her body and the psychic wounds Jonar's abuse had left, that she couldn't do this now without help.

"Gryphon can do this more effectively than you or any of your people," he informed her quietly. "I will send him up to sit with—"

"No men." She shook her head, almost violently. "Even our men don't go around her. Orders from Devlin. We don't mess with his orders, Dragon."

He sniffed impatiently. Human jealousy amazed him. It was not Devlin's directive; rather it had been Shanar, the

Savage, who had given that order. He would have to talk to that Viking soon. Lynn was exhausting herself.

"He does not have to be in the room." He finally shrugged. "I can have him positioned in the hallway..."

"Won't work." She shook her head again. "I can allow a male to work with me if the situation is dangerous enough to require it, such as yesterday. No men. No male power otherwise. Period. Let it go."

"You are exhausting yourself, Lynn." Dragon fought to keep his voice low. "This I will not allow."

Her slender shoulders lifted in a negligent shrug as she sipped at her coffee. She leaned her hip against the counter, watching him with a glimmer of amusement.

"You can't stop it." She seemed to derive great pleasure in this, Dragon thought with a frown.

"And you know this how?" He leaned forward as he held his coffee cup carefully between his hands, assuring himself he wouldn't become angry with the little spitfire.

She watched him warily. "Your code would refuse to allow you to stop me from any free choice I would make," she pointed out.

Dragon smiled slowly. "You have been talking to Devlin, of course." He nodded, thinking of the warrior who had just completed his claiming of the Earth Mistress. "In most cases he would be right. But there is one instance where my Dragon code can be overlooked and I may force my will on a single, special person."

Ah, yes, now she was looking decidedly worried. He liked having her off balance, wondering, uncertain what he would do.

She licked her lips slowly, nervously. "And that would be?"

He rose to his feet, abandoning his much-loved coffee for a hotter, spicier treat. He paced closer to her, staring down at her, ignoring her gasp as he lifted her from her feet and sat her on the cabinet. He stepped between her thighs, holding them apart, cursing the human cloth that separated him from her.

He caught her hands in his, pulling them behind her back and shackling them with his power as his head lowered.

"I can force my will on one person and one person alone." He allowed his lips to graze hers, his cock tightening at her strangled gasp of hunger.

"Who?" Her eyes were wide, a dark velvet brown, staring up at him with such innocence, with such aching need, he had to force himself not to take her then and there.

"I can do no other than protect the one who holds my heart," he told her before allowing his tongue to rim her parted lips in a long slow lick. "Should that protection be needed, then my code does not stand in my way. My code demands I protect, with my heart…" He nipped at her full lower lip. "…my soul…" He gloried in her moan of hunger. "…and to the fullest extent of my abilities, the life of my bond mate. You, little one, are the other part of my soul and this time, you will not escape me."

Dragon swallowed her cry as his lips slanted over hers, his tongue plunging into her mouth before she could deny the bond created so long ago. She strained against him, her breasts pressing into his chest as his hands tunneled into her hair, holding her head still as he plundered her mouth.

Her hard little nipples were like fire, piercing the skin cloth, burning into his flesh as her kiss burned into his soul. She moaned against his lips, her tongue twining with his, her thighs tightening on his legs as he ground the stiffened length of his cock against the heated pad of her sex.

He wanted to disintegrate the clothing she wore. He wanted to surge inside her, part the tight muscles of her cunt with his demanding erection and listen to her scream out her need for him.

His hands gripped her hips as the taste and heat of her kiss shattered reality around him. There was nothing but the two of them, their power flowing through their kiss, wrapping around their senses. If he didn't have her soon, he thought as he moaned against her lips, his hands pushing beneath her shirt, he would expire of lust. And it was beginning to appear that just such an end was what she had planned for him.

Chapter Nine

ഇ

Lynn was beginning to fear for her own sanity. There she sat, on her client's kitchen counter, her hands restrained behind her back and kissing Alyx as though she were dying for him. She *was* dying for him. The sensations spearing through her body were destroying all her preconceived ideas of sex.

She was restrained, unable to fight him, unable to move, and rather than pissing her off or terrifying her as it should, she was glorying in it. She had no control. Alyx controlled each touch, each move, and it was turning her on to the point that she was nearing orgasm from that sensation alone.

His lips covered hers with heated hunger; his tongue plundered her mouth and no matter how desperately she struggled to capture it with her own, he eluded her.

She thought the pleasure couldn't get any better. Then his hands moved to the hem of her tank top. His fingertips grazed the skin of her waist and cool air met hot flesh as he began to lift the material.

She moaned against his kiss, arching closer to him, her breasts trembling in anticipation of his touch. She shuddered in excitement. She might be restrained but she held every second of his attention for now. She knew. Knew every iota of his power and his mind was concentrated solely on her.

She knew she should be wary. Should be frightened. She could feel the strange power she feared so desperately moving stronger within her now, reaching out to Alyx. She clamped down on it, fighting to control it. But his kiss stole her mind, stole her strength.

Lynn couldn't help but cry out when his lips abandoned hers. She moved, reaching for him, needing more, needing his kiss as desperately as she needed oxygen.

"Look at you." The harsh, broken sound of his voice had her eyes opening, her heart racing at the intent, flushed expression on his face as he stared at her bared breasts. "So full and swollen. Your little nipples so pink and tempting they make me hunger as I never have before."

"Alyx, what are you doing to me?" He arched her back, lifting her breasts closer to him as his head lowered.

"I am having my morning meal," he groaned. "Sweet tender nipples and passion-ripe breasts."

His mouth closed on the tip of her breast as weakness flooded her entire being. Heat surrounded her nipple; a lash of moist, rough pleasure flayed it as he began to suckle at her hungrily. One hand cupped the firm mound, lifting it closer as the fingers of his other hand tweaked the nipple of its twin.

It was too much. Too much pleasure, too many sensations washing through her, ripping apart her control. She could feel his energy holding her up. Knew it was his because she was so damned weak there was no way she could have held herself up. All she could do was moan weakly, pleadingly, as he suckled her, rasped the sensitized nipple and sent flaming bolts of sensation spearing into her pussy.

Oh God, her cunt was so empty. She could feel the hollow ache there, the gripping need to be filled, to be taken. It was destroying her.

"Alyx, please." She arched closer to his tormenting mouth, her thighs tightening on his as she rubbed her sex against the hard ridge of his cock.

She didn't care how strange it looked, she needed it, wanted it now. She had to have him filling her. Fucking her. If he didn't soon she was going to go insane.

"Ask me." He was kissing her breast heatedly now, pushing the mounds together, his tongue licking from one nipple to the other.

His breathing was as hard as hers. His silvery eyes were dark, his long hair falling forward and creating a shimmering curtain of mercury around her breasts.

"Please, Alyx," she begged again, breathless, struggling against the coil of need tightening in her womb.

"Please what?" His voice was a raspy demand, desperate, filled with hunger.

"Oh God, Alyx, please…"

"Lynn, Zach is flying…oops…" The voice was a sharp intrusion, shocking Lynn, tossing her from the headlong flight into rapture and back into cold hard reality.

Alyx moved quickly, shielding her body, but it was too late. Face flushing, Liz turned and practically ran back through the swinging door as though the hounds of hell were riding on her ass.

"Fuck!" Alyx's curse ripped through the room at the sound of a helicopter overhead.

Instantly her wrists were released, her bra and shirt lowered and he was helping her quickly from the counter. She rested against his chest as she fought for balance, her mind whirling as the hunger seemed to eat her alive.

"Tonight." His hands tightened against her back as his body seemed to vibrate with intent. "Tonight, Lynn. I can wait no longer. Give me leave to come to you then. Quickly, Lynn."

"Tonight…" She shook her head, meaning to question the odd request.

"Tonight." He moved from her quickly. Before she could correct the misunderstanding, call him back, or deny what he seemed to be asking, he was gone. Just that fast. One minute he was there, the next he was gone.

"God, he has to stop doing that," she muttered, her voice as shaky as her body.

She vibrated with need. The feeling was like nothing she had ever known in her life, yet more than she wanted to admit. He wasn't human, she reminded her body desperately. Her body wasn't listening.

As she stood there fighting for control, a tentative knock came at the door. Lynn flushed in mortification. Thank God it was Liz who walked in on her and not one of the men. She was even more thankful of the fact that the psychic abilities the agents possessed weren't strong enough to pierce whatever shield Alyx had placed around them. Otherwise, Liz would have sensed what was going on behind the door and would not have entered.

"Come in. He's gone." She swiped her fingers through her hair and frowned.

Her hair felt a good inch longer than it had earlier. Maybe it was time to get it cut again.

"Sorry about that, Lynn." Liz entered the kitchen, her expression filled with wry amusement. "I didn't know…"

Liz pushed her shoulder-length black hair off her shoulder in a gesture of nervousness, while her dark blue eyes twinkled with warm amusement. She was one of the best agents on the force, and despite her slender build and exceptional good looks, got along well with all the men.

"Neither did I," Lynn muttered as she dragged in a hard breath. "Geez, Liz, that man is dangerous."

"Yeah." Liz smiled as she drew out the word. "I have to admit, he looked pretty damned determined. Pretty damned good, too." She laughed. "Sorry about the interruption, but Zach's helicopter just landed. I thought you would want to know." She shrugged regretfully.

"I will consider it a lucky rescue," Lynn breathed out roughly. "And thank God it was you bringing the message rather than one of the men."

"I don't know." Liz shook her head regretfully. "Maybe they could take lessons or something, Lynn. The world needs more of what you were getting there."

Lynn's blush heated her face as she stared at the other woman in shock.

"Bite your tongue," she hissed in mock reproof. "We've barely managed to convince them we can walk without an order to do so. We don't want them to know they actually have power over us."

Liz frowned in amused thoughtfulness. "Hmm. Okay. I'll go along with you on that, but I think you just want to save the good stuff all for yourself. Greed, Lynn, can be a bad thing."

They laughed as they left the kitchen, neither seeing the shadow that crept slowly along the floor, its intent the stairwell and the helpless woman sleeping above.

Chapter Ten

ഇ

"Devlin says they'll be arriving here in two more weeks." Zach was tired and cranky and Lynn could sense the worry tugging at his mind.

His full force of elite agents was concentrated in one area, making them an easy target for enemies desperate to rid the world of the good guys, Lynn thought.

Alyx and the two men who fought with him stood quietly on the far end of the study, their expressions intent, their hard faces impassive.

"I think we can let half the force here go, Zach," she told him as her brother finished running through the information he had brought with him.

His original trip had been a supply run. They weren't buying any groceries or supplies from the towns surrounding the estate, which meant everything had to be flown in personally.

"Good," Zach sighed. "We've had several calls come in and they're needed if you can spare them. But Miss St. James is high priority. Thankfully, she'll be under Devlin's protection soon."

Alyx shifted restlessly, drawing Lynn's gaze. She frowned. He didn't seem to be the restless sort.

"I'm still confused why they couldn't do this themselves from the onset." Lynn shook her head. "They're stronger than we are, in all ways."

Zach shook his head. "Devlin didn't say and I didn't ask. He's keeping an eye on things, though. If it gets too hairy, they'll come on in. I'd like to give him the time he needs. He wouldn't have asked for our help if it weren't important."

Lynn caught Alyx's movement from the corner of her eye. He was staring at the door to the study, his expression bordering on a frown, as though there were some confusion in something he was sensing. She couldn't feel anything. No hint of malice or darkness. Everything felt calm. Too calm, perhaps. The last two weeks had been one battle after another against the forces sent to take or kill Ariel. It felt strange, the sudden absence of the threat. Had they retreated so easily?

"Alyx and his men have made a difference." Lynn nodded to the three tense men.

Alyx stood taller, more imposing, but the others weren't lightweights. Gryphon was black-haired, with brilliant violet eyes. Phoenix was blond, with shimmering green eyes. All three were tall, bronzed and powerful. A lethal combination.

"Good." Zach nodded approvingly, his auburn hair falling over his brow as he frowned in irritation. He swiped it back, revealing a broad forehead and worried hazel eyes. "I'll take half of them back with me then— What the hell!"

The three men moved simultaneously, streaking for the door, throwing it back so violently it was torn from the hinge as they raced out of the room.

"Ariel!" Lynn screamed at the others in warning as she sprinted after the three warriors. "Liz, cover me. Jack, get ready to help."

As she ran she opened the door to her power, letting it surge fast and hard to the room down the hall. She didn't know how much time they had, and everything seemed to happen in slow motion. Her powers rushed through her, slamming into Ariel's room, creating a sense of vertigo as the misty impression of the bedroom lay over the real sight of her race up the hall.

The shadow was creeping for the bed, wide, menacing, a dark malevolent force that had somehow managed to slip past them all. She threw the astral shield over the restless form of the other woman; drawing on the sudden surge of power Liz threw at her and the stability Jack was providing.

It wasn't enough. She could feel the psychic force hammering at it, weakening it. She gasped painfully as the room seemed to fill with malevolent forces, weaving around them, seeking a way past their strength.

Then she felt it. The growing power she had kept so carefully in check. It strained against her control as the shield began to weaken further.

"Lynn, damn you to hell, stop fighting it," Alyx screamed out at her as he blocked the dark cloud snaking its way to the bed. "Protect her or we're all doomed."

The shield buckled further. The warriors had their hands full, their power blocking, fighting against the cloud of rage and fury fighting to get to Ariel. Around the bed, hated shifts of unnatural power whipped around them, probing at the cracks.

Gasping, almost frozen with fear, she eased open a fragment of the hold she had placed around the core of energy screaming within her. It flowed free. Hard, brutal, like a fist slamming into her mind as it finally merged within her being. Alyx. Herself. Whipping around her senses like an immature being, shrieking in joy.

Then it poured free. Astral screams of rage and pain resounded within her head as she drove the enemy's force back, strengthening the protective layers of power she had weaved around Ariel. She then worked on fighting back the attacking enemy as Alyx and his men worked at destroying the embodiment of hatred that filled the room.

Lynn had never seen anything like it before. Joining them, Zach added another layer of protection over Lynn's as they raced through the door to the sitting room and came to an abrupt stop. Alyx, Gryphon and Phoenix stood before the bed now, creating a shield around themselves and the dark cloud as it struck with a sudden, violent intensity.

This was no astral battle. She watched in amazement as the warriors countered the violent arcs of electricity with shields of energy and released their own from outstretched hands. They weaved about the area, bodies graceful in their strength, muscles bulging with the power it took to harness the incredible energy being used.

They blocked the dark force at each turn, moving it back, spearing into it with sizzling bolts of energy that produced horrendous shrieks of pain from within the cloud of evil. The warriors fighting it weren't doing so without risk, though.

Lynn watched as dark streaks of blood began to stain the cloth of the warriors' clothing. Alyx had a wide stripe across his bicep and the outside of his thigh. His face was strained as he held his arm outstretched, energy gathering as a brilliant ball of focused light in the center. His shield deflected a heated arc of flame as he aimed the spherical, psychic weapon and sent it flowing deep into the black mass.

Another shriek rent the air and the cloud seemed to shrink in size and menace. Gryphon and Phoenix, working in coordination with Alyx, aimed for the heart of the malevolent beast. The room rattled with the creature's scream of rage, the very air around them trembling in reaction to the power the warriors unleashed into the cloud. In the blink of an eye, golden light coalesced within its center, filling it, overtaking it, until it finally exploded in a shower of energy that washed over them all.

"What the bloody fuck was that?" Zach gasped as he collapsed to the floor, the power he had used to protect Ariel disappearing in a single instant. Liz fell next, cushioned by Jack's supportive arms as they breathed roughly.

Lynn reined her own power back, stumbling beneath the exhaustion of throwing everything she had into a shield that would protect the woman from the sinister threads of cloudy energy that had moved over them, searching for a weakness. She was weaker than ever physically, though the strength inside her seemed increased a hundredfold.

"Alyx." He stood tall beside the bed, his own wounds seeping slowly into the material of his black clothing.

He didn't appear harmed, but she could see the fine lines of weariness about his eyes and mouth now.

"Return to the ship," he barked at Phoenix, his eyes glowing with menace. "I want answers and you tell Koran I want them now or else all bets are off."

Phoenix disappeared just that quickly as Alyx swept Lynn into his arms, bracing her exhausted body against his own.

"Gryphon." He turned to the other warrior. "How severe are your wounds? I need you to protect the Wind Mistress."

"Shanar will get pissed," Gryphon sighed. "I'll protect the girl. My wounds are not as deep as your own and I'll heal quickly. Take your woman and rest."

The room seemed to spin around her, darkness threatening the edges of her mind.

"Alyx, what was it?" she gasped, as he lifted her into his arms and strode quickly from the room. "How did it get in here?"

She heard the growl of rage that vibrated in his chest and she shivered at the force of fury behind it.

"It is hatred, Lynn. Pure, unadulterated hatred sent by a force that has not been known of in over a millennia."

"But why didn't we sense it?" she asked weakly as he slammed the door closed on his bedroom, the dim, cool confines of the room washing over her in a wave of comfort.

"Because it's natural," he sighed as he laid her on the bed and sat beside her slowly. "Somehow Jonar has tapped into the dark force of this planet and harnessed its evil. Until the Shadow Warriors arrive and the crystal at Ariel's neck awakens, we can only play a game of wait and pray. Because it will be back. Hungrier and stronger than before."

Chapter Eleven

$\mathfrak{SD}$

Lynn protested weakly as Alyx stripped her of her clothing and tucked her naked between the sheets. Then she watched in amazement as he waved away his own clothing and proceeded to heal his wounds.

They appeared deep. Dark red blood stained his skin and he closed his eyes; a shimmering veil of energy enclosed him. As she watched, the wounds healed, but the effort it took to close them up left him pale and weak.

Afterward, he crawled into the bed beside her, pulled her against his larger body and slept. She needed desperately to follow him. She couldn't remember a time when it had taken so much of her power to hold back a force threatening one of her clients. Stopping bullets didn't leave her this drained.

The truly frightening part was that alone she could have never accomplished it. It had taken her, Zachary, Liz and Jack, backed by the entire force of psychics at their disposal, to shield Ariel and allow Alyx and his men the freedom to concentrate on keeping the evil from surrounding them. Had the alien warriors not been there, she knew they would have died in their effort to save the other woman, and it would have been in vain. She would have died with them.

Despite the weariness tugging at her, her mind refused to let her sleep. She had learned long ago that exhaustion this deep bred nightmares so horrible she would awaken gasping and crying out in pain. She never remembered the dreams. Never knew why her body ached as though a fatal blow had been delivered, but it terrified her. That fear held her awake now.

"Sleep, little love," Alyx murmured at her ear, his voice low and weary. "Nothing will harm you here. I promise you this."

His hands smoothed down her back, creating a firestorm of sensations that caused her to shiver in awareness of her state of undress.

"I will." She relished the feel of his strong arms surrounding her, the broad strength of his chest cushioning her head, the power of his thighs against her smaller ones. She had never been held so closely, with such warmth.

"When?" he grunted tiredly. "I cannot sleep while you are so tense and frightened, Lynn. I swear to you, that force cannot slip into this room. I have made certain that for the time being, we are protected."

"How?" They hadn't been protected from its invasion earlier.

He sighed deeply. "Are you certain you wish to know?"

"I asked, didn't I?" She frowned against his chest, stiffening further in his arms.

"I sent out a call to a friend," he said softly. "She will protect the area until Phoenix can return and lend his aid in doing so. We are safe. I swear this."

"And who's your friend?" She didn't like the bite of jealousy that struck at her. Help was help. Right?

"The friend was your Earth Mother." Amusement shaded his voice as though he were aware of the streak of jealousy. "It is her daughter we protect, just as it was the evil of her own planet that attacked. She will provide her protection until our strength is renewed once more."

Earth Mother? Mother Earth? Mother Nature? Lynn was certain she would be hysterical if she weren't so damned tired. She dealt with the paranormal on a daily basis. Knew of forms of evil that would break most men's minds. Fought the deadliest foes without knives or guns or fists and knew that true evil existed. Yet, the thought of being protected by a force she couldn't call upon, sense or see wasn't comforting.

"Alyx, I have to admit, this is getting too freaky, even for me." She breathed out heavily at the admission. "I thought I had seen everything there was to see that could terrify one human being. But I might have just reached my limit."

His arms tightened around her as he shifted against her. Her breasts raked against his chest, sending shooting darts of sensation through her nipples then straight to her pussy. She gasped at the pleasure, though her body felt heavy with exhaustion.

"If you do not go to sleep, I am going to spread your thighs and bring you to such a climax it will render you unconscious. If I do this then I promise you, Lynn, when you awaken, I will make you pay for the suffering I will go through waiting on your eyes to open. Trust me, you won't find it pleasant."

His voice was heavy with sexual warning, his cock already thick and hard, pressing between them demandingly.

"I can't sleep," she finally snapped. "I would if I could. But I can't."

"Why not?" His voice softened dangerously.

"Because I dream," she snapped, unwilling to face the dreams now that she had released the energy that had so begged to be free. "I'll have terrible nightmares and I'll awaken us both screaming, then you'll never rest. I'll nap until I catch up."

"I will protect your dreams." He sounded desperate now. "Close your eyes, little one, and sleep. I swear to you, no nightmares. I can do this, Lynn."

His cock pulsed against her stomach as he shifted again. Lynn gasped as it pressed harder against her.

"Can you sleep like that?" She didn't dare move away, look down or attempt to breathe too hard. She remembered clearly just how big and how strange it was. She still wasn't certain she would survive any sex act with him, though she was smart enough to know she would likely die trying.

"Sleep." The order was given in a hard, deadly voice.

Before Lynn could protest she lost all ability to think. Sleep slammed into her, dragging her into the dark, comforting well of utter senselessness.

Alyx breathed out in misery as he turned to his back, his cock jutting out in fiery demand as every breath Lynn took caressed flesh so sensitive it was torture to feel her and not take her.

He would never rest in this state, he thought wearily. His cock was like the monster she had seen it as, insistent once aroused, refusing to allow him rest or peace until he had given it at least partial satisfaction. Ahh, the trials and tribulations of being a Prime Warrior.

His hand wrapped around the broad length as the seminal fluid wept from the dual eyes at the tip. He stroked the lubrication along the demanding shaft, pulling Lynn tighter against his body; the feel of her, warm and sensuous, had a groan ripping from his chest.

He closed his eyes. He imagined the wet heat of her tight sheath and pumped the shaft with hard quick jerks of his wrist. He gritted his teeth as she moved against him, stroking his side, sending fingers of exquisite desire pouring over his body. His cock throbbed as his hips shifted, driving the length deeper into his fisted grip as a groan built in his chest.

He pumped himself harder, faster, the sensitive shaft and even more sensitive head streaking with heated ecstasy. His body tightened, his lips curling back from his teeth as his scrotum drew tight against his body, the veins along his erection throbbing, humming, the cock ridge twitching in building excitement until his orgasm washed over him with a nearly painful explosion of heated seed.

He was left gasping, nowhere near replete, and senseless with exhaustion. His eyes closed as he wrapped his power around the woman he held in his arms and sent a sharp, mental command to her unconsciousness to bring her a dream worthy of the sensual woman she was. A tired smile curled his lips. If he couldn't fuck her, the least he could do was up his chances that she would give in to him in her dreams.

As he allowed his own weary mind to rest a smile lifted his lips. She had given in to his power. The power he had given her soul so long before, she had finally released. She would be his now. Completely. Soon. They were bound and she would no longer be able to deny that bond. Finally, his mate was returning to him.

Chapter Twelve

∽

She had to see if that cock was real. Lynn felt a smile curve her lips as one of the odd, rare erotic dreams began to fill her mind. She usually existed in the world of nightmares when she slept. Visions of battles and blood, tears and remorse, had been her steady sleeping companions. But sometimes, as though Morpheus, the god of sleep, had found pity on her, she experienced one of the rare erotic treats she lived for.

And this treat was one she definitely needed to taste. Taste, touch, lick, suck. It didn't matter; she wanted it in her mouth. The need was like a hunger, building steadily, growing inside her, unable to control now that she had lifted the shield around that final force within herself.

Lynn sat up, suddenly awake, staring down at Alyx's sleeping body. She was breathing hard, blood surging within her veins, her juices seeping from her pussy, dampening her thighs. He was hers. She held a part of him forever within her. The dreams weren't dreams. They were memories. Another time, another life. She trembled at the thought. It wasn't easy to get used to. But she could get used to Alyx.

For all intents and purposes, he appeared no different from any other man she had ever known. Well, in shape anyway. He looked human, she amended, if a bit taller than most.

His flesh was a dark tanned hue; a toasty, warm color that suggested hours spent in the sun. Beneath the dark flesh, muscles rippled, corded with power in his broad chest. Tapering down, the impression of lean, finely tuned strength showed clearly in the hard packed abs, the sinewy strength of powerful thighs and long legs.

She swallowed tightly as her gaze skirted the most uncommon part of his body. It flickered back, then away. Finally, unable to resist, she gazed fully at the apparition he called a cock. The monster, he had dubbed it. The monster damned near suited it.

Even at rest, it was long and imposing, though not as thick as she had glimpsed the night she had walked in on him. She licked her dry lips nervously, staring at the ropy veins that pulsed under the flesh, wrapping over it in thick ridges as though the veins lay more above, rather than below, the skin. Her breathing became shallow as it seemed to twitch, and beneath the shaft his scrotum appeared to tighten.

She could clearly see the presence of not just two spherical balls, but three. She wanted to whimper as the massive organ began to harden, becoming erect in a matter of seconds, lifting from his hard stomach imperceptibly as though drawn to her.

There were two openings in the head of his cock, glistening with a film of slick moisture. If that wasn't disconcerting enough, beneath the head extended a thick, firm, rippled extension that looked more than menacing. The only problem was, she wanted to touch it. She should be terrified. She should have been scrambling to escape from what was sure to become a nightmare soon enough, but first, she wanted to touch it. Taste it. Suck it into her mouth and see for herself exactly how it felt. And she wanted to do it now.

Lynn ignored the trembling of her body as she moved carefully between Alyx's thighs. Kneeling before him, her hands reached for the straining flesh rising eagerly to greet her. She couldn't ignore the need anymore than she could ignore the power. Not any longer.

* * * * *

"Sweet Lynn." Alyx closed his eyes, gritting his teeth as her hands wrapped around his desperate erection.

His fingers tightened in the sheet beneath him, sweat forming on his brow as snaking arcs of sensation attacked his body in prickling chills. Her hands were as soft as satin, her fingers tentative, exploring, moving over the highly sensitive ridges of flesh along his shaft.

He felt her move. Knew what was coming. He breathed in hard and deep, wondering if he would survive it. The excitement alone would burst his heart at this rate. In his many years of life as a Prime Warrior, during all his deepest dreams, he had never imagined anything so sensual.

Her soft hands smoothed over the bulging head, fingers rasping the cock's crest just beneath it. The ultra-sensitive flesh rippled and tightened at her touch, causing his muscles to flex, his control to nearly evaporate as the pleasure wracked his body.

She hummed in approval as the long, hard ridges along the shaft of his cock throbbed at her touch. Pre-seminal fluid seeped from the dual opening at the tip, lubricating his cock, sensitizing it further.

"It's so big," she whispered, glancing up at him as his eyes opened, unable to keep from watching her.

Her delicate face was flushed, her shoulder-length brown hair a cloud of silk about her entranced expression.

"Lynn." He swallowed tightly. "Baby…" He was terrified of breaking the spell that seemed to wrap around them. Eroticism at its most heated, basic form.

"I want to taste you." Her voice was soft in the dim light of the room; the husky hunger filling it was like a whiplash of hunger searing him with its depth. "I've never done that, you know." Her hands slid up his cock, embraced the bulging head and crest before gathering his moisture and sliding back down.

His hips arched in reaction. His breath wheezed from his lungs as his balls tightened with the need for release. Hell. She was going to kill him.

"Never?" He fought to stay focused, to remain controlled. He knew he was fighting a losing battle.

"Never." She bent to him, pursed her lips and blew a gentle breath of air against the purpled head.

Alyx ground his head into the pillow, shaking, fighting the pleasure tearing through his body. Her innocence amazed him. Destroyed him.

"I'm going to suck it." She licked her lips, looking up at him from over the pulsing head of his cock, her expression devilish, full knowledge of her power over him glittering in her brown eyes.

"Lynn." He fought to keep his voice from resonating with the power gathering inside him. "Baby. You're not ready for this."

But he was. He was so ready to fuck her mouth he was about to come from the excitement of it alone. Despite the knowledge that she had opened her soul to him, he knew she hadn't fully admitted it to herself. She had given in to the power, nothing more. He would have felt it if it had been more.

She smiled. A second later a small, pink tongue slid between her lips, then tickled exploringly along the crested ridge under his cock head. Sweet mercy. He could feel his body tightening painfully as her hot tongue rode each hill and valley of the crest, licking over it, murmuring in appreciation of the taste she found there. Alyx was ready to scream out in an agony of suspended pleasure.

He could feel the Dar-phantom heating the stone at his chest in anticipation of this first ritual as pleasure seared every cell in his body. The crest was the most sensitive part of his erection, holding millions of live, sexual nerves pulsing under the thinnest shield of skin. It was a test of warrior control to hold back his ejaculation during stimulation of that particular area. He had never failed to last hours against the most practiced touch of the sexual trainers the Dragon Master had found. But now, beneath Lynn's touch, he was worse than an untried youth.

She came closer then, her lips opening, her tongue moistening the gentle curves. A second later, blistering velvet heat surrounded the tortured head and cock crest, drawing an agonized moan of pleasure from his straining chest. Her mouth was unlike any other sensation he had ever experienced.

She wasn't shy, either. She watched him, her gaze locked on his as he fought for control and she fought to take it. Her cheeks hollowed, drawing on him, sucking him nearly to her throat as his hoarse growl had her cheeks flushing.

"Lynn. Lynn." He shook in a wind of lust so forceful he felt his balls trembling with the need to release his seed. "Baby, listen to me, if you do this…" He gritted his teeth, desperate. God, he was such a fool. "If you do this, it changes you forever." The truth spilled from his lips. "You do this, baby. You change forever…"

His back arched as his hands tore the sheet beneath him, his heels digging into the bed as he fucked her mouth, dying at the thought of her releasing him. Cursing his own honor for needing to warn her.

She hesitated. Licked at the bulging tip and watched him heatedly.

"You've already changed me," she whispered.

The corners of her mouth held a fey little grin. He knew she thought she was aware of what his words meant. Thought he was merely talking about her power. It was power, but more. And he was dying.

Her lips tightened, her suckling intensified and his fears ceased to exist as he felt her tongue flickering quick, destructive little licks over the hyper-sensitive flesh. At the same time, the bulging head nearly touched her throat as the convulsive swallowing motion rippled over the flesh.

His hands moved, gripping her hair, holding her still. For a second, an infinite second, he fought to pull back, to force her from him, to explain... She swallowed again, her tongue stroked like silken lightning and he could no longer hold back.

The clamp of her mouth over his cock dragged as he thrust once, twice, then his victorious shout rocked the room. His semen exploded from the tip, filling her mouth as her eyes widened in sudden surprise.

"All of it," he cried out as he held her to him. "For mercy's sake, take it, Lynn. Take it all..." His seed pulsed to her throat and she accepted.

Power surged from his body, wrapping around them both, intense, bordering on pain, as she whimpered around his erection in alarm. But the bond had been met. The first ritual was completed. She had opened the door to her power and there was no closing it. Just as there was now no hiding from the mating of their souls. She had accepted. Knowledge was but the first step.

Chapter Thirteen

∞

"Alyx…" Lynn fought to breathe as she fell away from him, scrambling back on the bed, stumbling from the mattress as her flesh prickled, tightened.

She rubbed at her arms as she stared back at him in near panic. It was as though, suddenly, her body belonged to someone else. She could still taste the dark flavor of his seed in her mouth; feel the hum of his cock as he orgasmed. The sensation had traveled from her lips, her tongue, and now seemed to spread over her entire body.

He moved slowly from the bed. His silvery eyes glowed in the dark room as he moved with careful precision, stalking closer to her.

"Lynn, relax." His voice was too calm. Too soothing.

Hell. What did he do to her? She shuddered as a wave of sensation moved over her body. And it wasn't erotic. It was pinching, probing; fingers of power that seemed to dip into every cell and move under her flesh like a serpent burrowing to the bone. It didn't hurt, but it wasn't comfortable, either.

"Relax?" She fought to still the hysteria rising inside her. "You want me to relax?" She trembled convulsively as the snaking trails of heated power began to move through her body. "What did you do to me? Oh God. I knew this would be a bad idea," she moaned dreadfully. "Dumb, Lynn. Real dumb."

She didn't miss the faint grin that tugged at his lips.

"Do you often talk to yourself?" He countered her move to get to the door, crowding her back along the side of the bed.

"Only when I know the morons around me have no intention of helping," she snapped, her shoulders tightening as some sensation, a tickling pressure, seemed to press against her spine. "What did you do to me? What the hell did that monster spurt down my throat?"

There was no sense blaming him. She clearly remembered his warning. But no. Did she listen? Dumb-ass Lynn had just carried on, sucking his cock like it was her favorite dessert and she couldn't get enough. Well, it was packing more than calories, that was for damned sure.

Oh hell, why had she just *assumed* she knew what he was talking about? Why hadn't she just let him explain?

"Lynn, it's okay." There was that tone again. She narrowed her eyes on him as she retreated further.

He was too damned big. Too powerful. And he seemed intent on hemming her in.

"You come one step further and you'll be snacking on the monster's jewels." She pointed her finger at him demandingly, watching as he slowed, stopping at the end of the bed.

"Women always want to go for the balls," he sighed, shaking his head. "Let me hold you, Lynn. I can help."

"Help?" She was going to need help? She swallowed tightly. "Why do I need help?"

He tilted his head, the thick silver of his hair flowing over one broad shoulder.

"I can make it less frightening," he suggested. "It's merely a joining, baby. A merging..."

She rubbed desperately at her arms. She could feel her skin flexing, protesting whatever was moving beneath it.

"You can do that by making it stop," she demanded, ignoring any attempt at an explanation. She didn't want a joining. She wanted it to stop. "Make it stop now, Alyx." She fought the panic she could hear building in her voice, rising in her body.

This was not happening. She was not going to freak out here. Whatever it was, it was natural. Had to be natural. She was not going to have a breakdown over this. But she knew she had never heard of any of her friends describing such a reaction after giving a really hot blowjob. And they would have told her, too. No, this wasn't in any way natural. It was as though the power she had released earlier was now finding form, swirling within her body like another, separate entity.

"Lynn, it won't stop." Lynn was certain he had somehow moved closer, but she was damned if she had seen him move.

"Oh yes, it better stop." She stared at him imperiously. "It is going to stop. Make it stop now."

"It doesn't work that way, baby." He shook his head slowly; that grin tilting his lips was too knowing, too smug. Dammit. It was always a bad sign when a man looked smug.

"What is it?" Why did she have a bad feeling she was going to regret asking that question?

"It's knowledge." His voice deepened, his eyes darkening.

Knowledge, her ass! Lynn wanted to gape at him but she was too busy trying to fight the sensation of another presence moving through her body.

"I knew I would regret asking." She felt her stomach tighten in dread. "So what the hell is knowledge?" She jumped as a sharp pinching sensation at the base of her spine preceded a wave of heat streaking up it. "Oh, hell.

This isn't funny, Alyx." She tried to reach back, to slap at the stinging area, terrified of what she was going to find there.

"Easy, Lynn." He caught her in his arms before she could stop him.

Pulling her against his chest, his body heat warming her, his hands running up and down her back gently, he whispered at her ear. "It is merely my force. My power. I told you, we are two parts of a whole. Somehow, your unconscious mind, the power you gave freedom to, has accepted this as you accepted my release. It is merely a ritual. A binding..."

Oh, no. This was not happening. She wasn't bound to anyone, let alone some silver-eyed, wicked-tongued alien. Nope. Not in this lifetime.

Lynn tore herself from his embrace. "No." She moved across the bed, stumbling, weak, but managing to stay on her feet as she hit the floor and stooped down to grab her clothes. "I acknowledge nothing," she yelled back at him as she jerked her shirt over her head, struggled with her jeans. "Do you hear me, Alyx? Nothing. So make it stop."

He crossed his arms over his chest, his expression settling into lines of mockery, the monster standing stiff and erect in front of his body. Oh God, were those eyes watching her? The dual slits in his cock were damned unnerving.

He shrugged as she watched him, fury surging through her body. "I can stop nothing, Lynn. Your soul has acknowledged mine. The release of my seed was merely a catalyst. I cannot undo it. I would not undo it even if it were possible."

Fury overwhelmed her. Fury at him, at herself. She didn't want this. Dammit, whatever was happening to her was scaring the hell out of her. It was too freaky. Suddenly her body wasn't her own. Her psychic power wasn't strong enough to force the invader out of her and it was doing things to her she couldn't explain.

"Your own powers will become stronger…"

"Yeah, I needed more of that psychic crap tormenting the living hell out of me," she snapped as she jerked her jeans over her hips and buttoned them jerkily.

She ignored his surprised look, the hurt that seemed to flash in his eyes.

"It was to protect you," he said quietly. "It was not to be a burden you had to bear."

"Well surprise, big boy," she told him furiously. "If I could rid myself of it, I would. Do you think I like knowing how evil men can be? Do you think I enjoy fighting them? Do you think for one minute it's been pleasant trying to adjust to things no human should ever have to face alone?"

"Your brothers were there to aid you…" He shook his head as though suddenly uncertain of the choices he had made so long ago.

"Brothers. Oh, they love it," she snarled. "They get to play tough asses in a way few men can. But let me tell you right now, Alyx. I don't like it, and I sure as hell don't want more."

His shoulders straightened. His expression hardened into lines of cold, hard determination. "You are alive. Do you deny it has saved your life on more than one occasion?"

"Big fucking deal. It was the stupid powers that put me in danger to begin with," she pointed out loudly. "What the hell good is alive, Alyx, when I can't enjoy my life?"

"At least you are not dead." The room seemed to vibrate with his rage, shocking her to silence. "Alive is not lying in a battle field, dying in my arms again. Alive is not taking your last breath as I feel your sorrow that you had not taken the gifts I would have given you. Damn you, Lynn. It's surviving until I could find you."

The dreams. Nightmares. They burst through her mind then like a rainbow of shattered glass. Blood and death. Sorrow and rage. And her own foolishness. She was berating him, blaming him, when it was her fault for not accepting. Her fault for hiding for so many years. She had been worse than a child afraid of the monsters under her bed. Afraid, instead, that the monsters were inside her.

She backed away from the bed, moving for the door, fighting the fiendish visions that tore at her skull. Fighting the knowledge that he had once been everything to her. It was there. Like a sharp blinding light, tearing through her consciousness. He had been her heart. Her soul. And once again she was denying him.

"Lynn, wait." His voice was commanding, harsh, as she reached the door.

She groped for the doorknob, twisting it violently as she jerked the door open. "I can't think like this. With you," she cried out desperately. "I can't stay. I can't. Just leave me alone, Alyx. For now. Just leave me alone."

She turned from him and rushed from the room, flinching at the violence of the door slamming, the fury behind the sound. She kicked at the wall, screeching in fury at the unaccustomed pain in her bare feet.

Chapter Fourteen

ß∂

Okay. She was hysterical. Panic was a forgotten memory. She had passed that phase as she stood before Alyx and heard the shattering pain in his voice as he described her nightmares. Nightmares he had experienced. Nightmares he said had already played out.

She sat on the balcony outside her room, staring into the night, feeling a surge of strength in powers she had finally accustomed herself to. She had become comfortable with the strength of her powers. They rarely fluctuated, and after learning how to harness what she had, they never surged as they had in her youth.

Now, she only wished surges were all she had to deal with. Her flesh was suddenly supersensitive. The slightest breeze was like the firmest caress. She didn't like this. She was wearing clothes. They shouldn't feel like a layer of sand scraping over her skin. Her toes shouldn't feel like they were being singed by the warmth of her sneakers. Yet, barefoot, the lightest step was like pins prickling at them.

"This is not a good thing," she muttered to herself as she stared up at the clouds marring the black velvet sky. "Lynn, couldn't you have found another way to get your ass into more trouble?"

She sighed wearily. She hadn't been nice to Alyx. There was no excuse for it, not really. Just because he had done this creepy thing with the power building through her body didn't mean she had to be cruel.

It was her own fault, she charged herself mockingly. She hadn't been asleep when he orgasmed. She had heard his warning. Had felt the sense of impending disaster building in her stomach, but she had been too drugged by the desperate response from Alyx's body. She had held him spellbound. Her. Quiet little Lynn who had never really held anyone spellbound without cheating, had held this big tough, larger than life alien with only the warmth of her mouth.

She had disregarded the fact that the man had a cock that would terrify even the most jaded prostitute.

"Hell, is it even a cock?" she muttered to herself.

"Of course it is." She shook her head as she rolled her eyes at such a thought. "Has to be. Please let it be." Her desperate whimper of feminine arousal would have been laughable under any other circumstances, she thought.

"Fine," she growled quietly, the sound of her own voice strangely comforting as she tried to work through yet another paranormal upheaval in her life. As though she needed more. "It was definitely a cock. Now, just gotta figure out the antidote before my skin starts shedding like a damned snake." She was itchy, uncomfortable, and she would be naked if it weren't for the fact that even oxygen irritated her skin.

"Dragon will bring you skin cloth, I am sure." The voice echoed from the darkness, causing her to squeal in surprise as she jumped from her chair and turned to face the intruder.

Gryphon stood across from her, his long black hair flowing around his shoulders as he watched her curiously.

"What the hell are you doing out here?" she snapped, grimacing as the pads of her feet protested the feel of the shoes covering them.

"Were you not talking to me?" he asked her with some confusion.

The moon decided to peek from behind the covering of the clouds then, casting a golden ray of light across his face, making his violet eyes glitter eerily. What was with those eyes? Dragon's seemed to glow as well, like deep, rich mercury.

"No. I wasn't talking to you." She tried not to snarl or to flush in embarrassment. "I was talking to myself."

He frowned. "You do this often then? Talk to yourself?"

"Yeah, I do," she growled sarcastically. "It's the only damned way to get a halfway decent answer back."

He shook his head.

"Speak with Alyx. He is quite intelligent. I'm certain he can assure you he does indeed have a cock." The droll answer had her gritting her teeth in anger.

"Ha ha." She sneered. "Go crawl back under your rock now and let me just muddle along on my own." She flicked her fingers toward the door he had come through.

Shaking his head, Gryphon leaned against one of the beams that supported the roof of the porch.

"Are you always such a disagreeable woman?" he asked her softly, supposedly seriously.

"Yeah. I am." She sat back in her chair, suddenly weary, suddenly realizing she was just that. Very disagreeable.

"Your brother and the males you work with seem very intelligent as well," he said gently. "Why do you not speak to them rather than yourself?"

Why didn't she? Lynn shook her head. "They wouldn't understand," she finally sighed. "Hell, I don't understand it myself."

She didn't like change. She didn't like surprises. The paranormal gifts she lived with daily were often difficult to handle. The emotions and sensory changes that attacked her kept her off balance, her system rioting.

"Sometimes..." Gryphon spoke carefully. She could *feel* him choosing his words and she hated it. "Sometimes, a soul, a human soul, is given a special gift by one capable of sharing his or her powers. If that human's physical body dies, the soul retains that gift into the next life. It retains it for a reason. Because the soul of that person knows what their mind often does not."

Lynn stared up into the sky once again and sighed heavily.

"We would first have to agree reincarnation exists," she pointed out, though she knew she was already accepting that fact.

"To do that, we would have to forgive a past we do not remember, and yet cannot forgive ourselves for," he murmured. "All things come full circle, Lynn. Look into the knowledge that allowed you to accept the power reaching out to you. Look into the nightmares you fight and forgive yourself for something you could not change. Then, and only then, will you be able to accept who you are, and the gifts you were given."

But she had failed. In those nightmare images, that knowledge had remained uppermost. That despite her strength, her training, her loyalty, she had failed. The person she was sworn to protect had died.

"How can you know that?" Her hands gripped the arms of the chair, uncomfortable with the fact that she could feel every bump and groove in the plastic.

He sighed deeply. "One day, you will have the answer to that. But it is an answer you must find within yourself."

"I don't believe in reincarnation," she snapped confrontationally.

His chuckle was warm, amused. "Do you not? Why do you fight it so hard then? Why were you so desperate to cut Dragon with your sharp tongue if you do not believe? Ask yourself this, Lynn. If your visions are based in truth, what then has Dragon suffered?"

His scream echoed through her soul. Lynn flinched, a muted whimper of protest escaping before she could contain it.

"When a warrior gives of himself to his bond mate," Gryphon continued, "and his bond mate refuses him, a part of his Dragon stone dies as well. It is this stone that sustains him while away from our world. It is his companion until the final ritual between him and his bond mate. His solace. His strength. If that mate is taken from him, then he loses that as well. He either returns forever to our home world, or he suffers the darkness of complete solitude within his soul. Something that no warrior should know."

Lynn shook her head quickly. "I don't want to hear this."

"Why?" His voice was mocking, soft. "It is hard, is it not, to face another's pain? This is why you curse the very gifts that have saved your life countless times. Because staying apart, holding yourself isolated from the pain of loss, is so very hard when you can sense every emotion in the very air around you. And you would curse Dragon as well, for allowing you the strength to survive those who would have taken you from him again, before he could have found you."

"You're wrong." But there was no heat in her protest. No way to convince others when she couldn't even convince herself now.

"Perhaps I am." She grimaced as she felt his shrug disrupt the air.

"Don't do that," she snapped before she could stop herself as she felt the disturbance in the air from his movement. She groaned in misery. "How do I stop this?"

"Cease to care," he told her mockingly. "Is that not what you want anyway, Lynn? Complete disassociation? Or, accept the next gift Dragon will bring you. And the completion of the bond."

She glanced at him again in surprise. "What do you mean?"

This time, it was Gryphon who shook his head. "Something else you must learn on your own, Lynn. If you are strong enough to care." It was a carefully worded dare.

Lynn snorted. "Just like a man."

"Yes." Smug amusement filled his voice. "Many of us are much alike, no matter the universe which spawned us. Our benevolent God knew perfection when He created it."

"Oh really," she drawled. "I hold with the thought that men were the rough draft, women the perfection. He knew He messed up when He made man."

Gryphon chuckled. "At least you do not deny us the belief of Him. Many would."

Lynn shrugged. "I've heard He works in mysterious ways." She contained her smile.

"That He does." Gryphon sighed. "I will leave you, then, to carry on the discussion you were having with yourself. Perhaps if you try honesty, though, the answers might come more easily."

"You know, Gryphon, I really don't think I like you," she said tiredly. "When a man starts making sense, it's time for a woman to have her own head examined."

"Or for her to realize it is time to listen," he suggested instead. "Good night to you, Lady Lynn. Try resting in the bed, in the nude. The silk sheets on your bed are the closest you will get to skin cloth. It could help until Dragon returns."

"He's gone?" she asked, surprised.

Gryphon paused at the door into Ariel's sitting room. "For a while." His voice was too soft. Too somber. "Just for a while."

Chapter Fifteen

🔊

It was nearly dawn before the door to her bedroom opened and Dragon entered the dim room. Lynn wasn't asleep. She was staring at the ceiling, slowly accustoming herself to the sensitivity of her skin and the changes she could sense moving around her. It was as though her very flesh were absorbing the nuances of emotion and psychic energy flowing through the house.

She could feel Ariel's body healing, the crystal charging. Slowly. Too slowly for her peace of mind. She could feel her brother's concern. She knew it was him. He was pacing his room, concerned about her, but hesitant to disturb her. She could feel the others as well. Differing emotions, not really clear, but disturbing all the same.

When Dragon stepped into the room and closed the door behind him, she saw the determined set of his shoulders, the cool resolution in his glittering silver eyes, and she knew that the time for any denial was at an end.

She watched him still as he closed the door, his gaze darkening as it went over her naked body. She knew what he was seeing. She was flushed, sensitive. Her breasts were firm, her nipples peaking beneath his gaze. Could he sense her arousal? Had he always sensed his effect on her?

"I won't regret giving you the power needed to keep yourself safe until this moment." His voice was hard, chillingly resolute. "It is perhaps not the life you would have wished..."

"Alyx. I'm sorry." She couldn't bear to hear the somber pain in his voice. "I was mildly upset earlier. I rarely react well when my flesh starts crawling."

He moved closer to the bed as he laid some dark material in the chair by the door.

"If I take you, the connection becomes stronger," he warned her. His silver eyes glowed with lust; his body tightened with it.

She could tell he really wanted to take her. The monster was like a swollen ridge rising from between his thighs, pressing against the strange material of those pants he wore.

"I can't live like this," she sighed tiredly. "It was bad enough before, when my own dreams mixed with those of the people around me, creating nightmares I couldn't hide from. Now I can *feel* those nightmares, Alyx. I can feel the pain..."

"I can fix this, Lynn." He stood by her bed, staring down at her.

His gaze was hot enough to send fire flickering over her body. Her nipples engorged further, as though reaching out for him. She wanted to feel his mouth on her. She *could* feel his mouth on her. She gasped at the sensation of wet heat surrounding the puckered tip.

"You can feel my desires, unless I block them from you." His voice was wicked carnality. "The things I could do to you, with only a thought, would be more pleasure than you can imagine. But you could do the same to me, Lynn. As your powers mix with mine and begin to develop, control will come. The skin cloth will protect you from others, absorb their impact, store the power for when you would need it. Our life is not as bleak as you would believe it is."

"You're changing the rules of my world," she whispered sadly. "I was just getting used to them, Alyx."

"Watch." His voice deepened. Lynn's eyes widened.

The black clothing he wore seemed to part, as though ripped from his body by an unseen hand, and fell to the floor at his feet. The black shirt that fit perfectly over his muscular chest, the snug pants and soft-looking boots, all gone. Bending down, he picked them up. Lynn's eyes widened as he held it before her. It was intact. As though he had undressed himself with the greatest of care. He tossed them to the chair.

Lynn made a mental note to question what she had just seen. Later. Definitely later. With his nudity came a tidal wave of sensations that had her arching in exquisite pleasure. Not exactly a physical touch, it was as though need breathed, whispered, and each sigh of longing stroked her flesh.

"Oh God. Have I mentioned I hate the paranormal?" She twisted beneath the psychic caress.

"I believe you may have mentioned this a time or two." He lowered himself to the bed beside her. "Have I mentioned how much I have longed for you? How I have awaited this day?"

He lay on his side, his hand moving, fingers stroking up her stomach, moving with delicate heat to run around her breast. Lynn's breath caught. As though his presence blocked any other external waves of power, the only sensations now were those of his touch, his lust.

"I'm going to be upset later," she assured him with a gasp, her body arching, nearly peaking with pleasure as he blew a heated breath over her turgid nipple. "Much later."

She didn't give him time to reply. She turned in his arms, her lips finding his, her moan echoing around her at the banquet of tastes and sensations she found in his kiss.

He took her lips the moment they met his. Oh God. She felt her womb clench as his tongue speared into her mouth, twining with hers, his lips masterful, dominating. His arms wrapped around her, pulling her against the hard muscle of his body, his cock nudging between her thighs as he bent to her.

Oh, yes. This was good. Her hands clenched in his hair as he possessed her mouth. His lips moved over hers with an expertise that left her gasping, begging for more. It was so good. Too good.

Lynn twisted in his grip, her thighs opening for him, hips writhing to press her hungry cunt against the wide head of the monster. He felt so good. So warm and incredibly sexy. And her flesh seemed to eat up every touch of his skin against her. As though the very pores were soaking in the essence of him. She twined her arms tighter around his shoulders, reveling in the feel of strong male muscle and heated sensuality. He stretched along her, covering her body, his elbows holding the better part of his weight from her. She wanted that weight. Wanted him pressing her into the mattress, wanted his skin kissing hers just as his lips were.

She was becoming drunk on the taste of him. Like spiced brandy, hot and intoxicating, his tongue tempted her to take more. To take and take until she could find some sense of satiation. Yet somehow, she knew she never would.

"No," she whimpered as he pulled away, his lips stroking down her neck, his tongue licking over her skin as he murmured his pleasure.

"Yes," he growled at her shoulder, his big body shifting as he continued lower. "I want to taste you, Lynn. All of you. I want to know every scent, every flavor of your flesh. I want to devour you, Lynn."

Her womb clenched at the hard, rough sound of his voice. It was graveled, a raw, primal sound that stroked over her senses like pure sin. Dark and velvety, tempting, addictive.

Lynn licked her dry lips, her hands clenching at his shoulders, back arching as his lips began to trail seductively around the curve of her breast. Rough satin was the only way to describe the feel of his lips as they stroked closer and closer to her nipple. Heated, with just enough friction to remind her they could harden at a second's notice. The damp warmth of his tongue peeked out, licking over the swollen curve he moved along.

Anticipation heightened every nerve in her body. She was straining toward his mouth before it ever enveloped the hard, throbbing nipple.

"Alyx." She couldn't halt her cry, or the reflective jerk of her body as pleasure flayed her from her nipple to her womb.

Her vagina clenched its own hungry demand as her fingers locked in his long hair, holding him tighter to her as he began to suckle the nub of flesh he held. His teeth gripped the tender tip; his tongue stroked it until she was a writhing mass of desperate sensations.

Alyx's hands weren't still, either. He held himself above her with one arm, his hand clenched in her hair, holding her still as he tormented her. The other smoothed down her waist, gripped her hip for a second before continuing to her thigh.

He shifted, moving his mouth from one breast to the other, lifting his hard abdomen from between her thighs and replacing it with his hand. Lynn stilled, panting for breath, held suspended on such a rack of intensity she wondered if she would survive it. He was flaming lust, incredible gentleness, and all hard, sensual male.

His fingers parted the swollen lips of her pussy as she fought to breathe. His tongue licked her nipple with raspy demand, then his fingers were sliding along the silky, cream-filled slit to the hard button of her clit.

She nearly rocketed through the ceiling. Her back arched as a strangled cry tore from her lips. Her hands clenched tighter in his hair as feathery strands caressed the curves of her breasts. Staring down at him, she watched his eyes glow, the outer sapphire ring more striking now than ever before.

His head raised, his eyes still locked with hers.

"There are three phases of bonding," he whispered. "You have knowledge now. Of who I am. What I am. The power we share as one. When I take you, when your body imprisons mine, you enter acceptance. Where your soul accepts the knowledge it's been given, just as your body accepts, there can be no pleasure greater than what you find in my arms. The third is completion. Binding us forever, Lynn. You cannot escape the third if you carry through with the second."

Lynn knew she should have been terrified. She should be screaming. Fighting. She should have left the first day he arrived. But she wasn't about to lie to herself now. She had already come too far to ever back away.

She bit her lip as his fingers rolled around her clit then. A soft, silken slide of flesh that had her pussy creaming in excessive need, her hips arching for a firmer stroke, an end to the pulsating demand that tormented every cell in her body.

"Too late," she moaned, her head twisting on the bed. "It's already too late, Alyx. Please. I can't stand it much longer. Let the monster have its way or go ahead and shoot me and put me out of my misery."

He laughed with sinful darkness. "How about I do both?"

He rose to his knees in a fluid, graceful movement that left her gasping. Keeping her legs spread, he lifted them until they draped over his thighs, the lips of her cunt cushioning the hard tip of his cock. But he would go no further. He stared down at her, watching her as she arched her hips, a plea trembling on her lips.

"Touch yourself." He gripped her hand, lowering it to her straining clit. "Let me see you, Lynn. Let me watch as you pleasure yourself."

She felt her juices flowing from her pussy now, covering the broad flesh pressed against the tender entrance. Tentatively, her fingers moved on cream soaked flesh, circling the straining bud of her clit as she whimpered in agonizing arousal.

It was too much. Too damned intense. He had her poised on the edge of an explosion she doubted she would ever recover from. Yet she was meeting it willingly.

She could barely hold her eyes open. Barely breathe. Yet she stared up at him, her gaze locked with his as she gasped, each breath strangled with sensation as her fingers stroked over her own flesh and his cock throbbed at the portal to her cunt.

"Yes," he hissed as she felt the sensations building, moving just under her skin like a separate entity, greedy now for the explosive pleasure to come. "How pretty you are. Your fingers wet with your own juices, your face flushed and hungry for me. Make yourself come for me, baby. Give your little clit its release and I'll give you what you hunger for."

His voice sent her over the edge. Her fingers moved around the little bud, faster, firmer, until her womb was pierced with a rapture that sent it spasming with strong, rhythmic convulsions of release. She arched, crying out weakly, then breathing was forgotten entirely as his cock pierced her pussy.

Her eyes widened, dazed. She could feel each ridge stroking into her. Firm, flexible, vibrating with a steady throb of need as it stretched her, filled her, tearing through the shield of her innocence even as the pleasure ripped through her sanity.

She could feel the cock crest, like tiny fingers caressing the very depths of her pussy. Stroking with devilish, teasing tips of silken, erect flesh. The heavy ridges pulsed, vibrated, even as he began to stroke inside her with a deep, powerful rhythm.

"Alyx?"

Her legs were bent over his thighs, spread wide as he stared between them. His eyes were narrowed, his expression savagely intense as he watched his cock burrow in and out of the slick tunnel it possessed.

The sound of wet flesh meeting, suckling greed and penetrating pleasure wrapped around her. Her senses were dazed, her nerve endings so alive that each breath was a caress, each sigh a nearly orgasmic experience. She could feel every nuance of his erection as he pushed inside her slowly, forcing his way past ever tightening muscles, only to pull back and begin again.

Each thrust sent electrical impulses snaking through her body, wrapping around her clit, convulsing her womb as her greedy body arched, searching for more. She was shaking, trembling as she teetered on the edge of climax.

"More," he groaned, and forged deeper.

Lynn mewled desperately, her hands reaching beneath her legs to clench on his thighs, to find a stable base, something solid to anchor her to Earth. He was taking her harder now, plunging into her forcefully as the world began to collapse around her.

His hands gripped her thighs, nearly bruising in their intensity as he began to fuck her harder, deeper. She could feel the broad head pressing against her womb, throbbing heatedly as he groaned above her. Her back bowed, driving her cunt down harder on the plunging cock, her muscles tightening further, her senses reveling in the pleasure/pain the action sent flooding through her body.

She panted for breath, her vision darkening as she felt the coil of heat in her belly begin to tighten. Harder, faster, his cock slammed into her vagina and she accepted every desperate plunge with hungry gasps and imperative need as her pussy began to heat, spasm, shooting impulse after impulse into the hard knot of sensation centered in her womb.

She exploded in a blinding flash of light that would have put the Fourth of July celebration to shame. Stars exploded in her head as her muscles bore down on his driving cock, her pussy flooding with her release, her body straining against the tidal wave of incredible pleasure suddenly flooding her system.

Power surged, erupting through her pores, pouring toward him like a wave of pure, clean energy. She could feel it, sense it ripping through her body even as her orgasm destroyed her. And she knew in that moment where it would center. In the Dragon stone he wore. In the heart of his power. And for a second, only one blinding incredible moment, she wanted nothing more than to flow along with it as she felt him shudder, his cock pulse, a hard throb, then the searing blasts of his seed as it flooded her pussy. Returning the power. The thought was hazy, distant, as she screamed out his name, exploded again then collapsed wearily to the bed.

Chapter Sixteen

ஒ

Lynn had to admit, sex with Alyx was the best damned thing she had ever known in her life. But, it was also the most confusing. No more than minutes after his desperate release into her body, she began to feel small, subtle changes. An intensity in her own power, as though it were finally coming to a focal point, rather than zipping around aimlessly in her body.

She lay there, frowning, staring up at the ceiling as he breathed heavily beside her, his arm across her waist, anchoring her to the bed. She could feel him. Not just physically, but psychically, as though he were a part of her soul now.

"What just happened?" She was amazed at the calmness of her voice as she finally asked the question.

Alyx stiffened beside her. "You don't like the paranormal, remember?" He chided her need for answers.

His arm moved, his hand flattening over her abdomen, fingers smoothing over her dampened skin.

Lynn sighed, pressing her lips together somberly before speaking. "I hate being out of control, Alyx. The power is never stable. Never truly mine to control. I can hold it for a while, but it's never steady. And I'm always frightened." That was the hardest part to admit. That fear.

His fingers stilled. He lifted himself on his elbow until he could rise beside her, staring down at her questioningly. She glanced away, terrified of seeing the condemnation in his eyes that she had seen in others countless times before.

Alyx lifted his hand from her stomach, cupping her chin and turning her head until his gaze held hers once again.

"If I had died on this planet, before finding my bond mate and sharing the power I gave her so long ago, then I would have been as a wraith. Here, but not here. Forever searching, never finding. Knowing that in your hour of need, when danger surrounded you, I could not aid you. I would have been forced to watch your death each time your spirit was reborn, for daring to tamper with the natural order of life and bond mates. I know fear, Lynn. Every battle, every fight; I have known fear."

Her eyes widened in surprise. There was no condemnation; there was only acceptance in his silver gaze.

"I knew you were out there," she whispered. "You terrified me, Alyx, before I even knew who you were. Accepting this isn't easy for me."

But she had accepted it. She knew that now. Accepted the bond they shared. Accepted the fact that somehow, somewhere, she had known and loved him before.

"I have always searched for you, Lynn." He smoothed her cheek with the backs of his fingers before outlining her lips with his thumb. "You would not accept what I had to give you in that earlier life. I could not force it on you. Now, though, you will be protected."

Lynn frowned. Her nightmares were of blood and death. Of regret.

"You can't protect me from death, Alyx," she sighed tiredly. "It's always waiting."

"Not any longer."

Her heart jumped in her chest as she stared up at him. Flinty determination filled his eyes now.

"What have you done?" She knew for a fact she didn't really want to know this time.

"Nothing too upsetting yet," he growled as he pushed himself away from her. "The Completion can not be attained without your full acceptance, Lynn. When you accept, then it can begin."

He sounded angry, but she knew him now. She was just as much a part of him as he was of her. She couldn't share his thoughts, but there were suddenly things she sensed, knew about him, that she couldn't explain.

"I can't accept it without knowing what it is." She sat up, realizing her skin was slowly regaining the sensitivity it had felt before.

He stiffened, his broad back rippling as his muscles tensed before her.

Alyx glanced back at her, his gaze hooded, sparking with emotion.

"And when you know, you will perhaps never accept." He snorted.

Lynn rolled her eyes. "Now that really makes sense, Alyx. Why do men always have to be so confusing?"

"Is this another of those questions you ask only of yourself?" he asked her darkly. "Or do you really expect an answer?"

"Might as well ask it of myself." She rubbed at her arms as she glanced toward the balcony doors. The sun was rising, bathing the land around them with warmth.

She needed to shower and dress before helping Ariel into the bath and getting her breakfast. The other woman was growing much stronger after her ordeal at Jonar's hands, but she was still incredibly weak.

"Here." He rose to his feet and walked to the chair. "You will wear this."

When he turned back, she saw the clothing in his hands. She was ready to make a cutting remark about the color black when she happened to look into his eyes. He was expecting it and was steeling himself against the pain.

The black skin cloth, as Gryphon has called it. Identical to the clothing the warriors wore. Her brow creased into a frown. Why did she have a feeling that once she donned those clothes she would never be the same again?

"I kept it as simple as possible." He laid the clothing on the bed along with a pair of incredibly soft-looking calf boots. "Yours buttons. When you decide you no longer want or need the inconvenience of the buttons, then the cloth will conform to that. But you must wear it, Lynn. It will be your only defense against the absorption of psychic resonances through your skin. Later, I will teach you how to soak in the energy. But for now, you need first to accustom yourself to the increased power."

She breathed in deeply. "Can I shower, at least?"

He smiled slowly. The curve of his lips was pure, indulgent carnal intention.

"You will love the shower now, darling. In ways you could never imagine."

Great. Now she would have a shower fetish as well as an alien fetish. Not just an alien, but an alien with a monster cock. Lynn shook her head. If this day became any weirder she might just hang it all up, go to bed and refuse to come out for weeks. Of course, she would have to have Alyx with her.

She shook her head at that thought. She may as well admit she was a goner. She was in love with him. And that was the most frightening revelation to date. She had only known him a few days, but he already filled her heart more fully than his cock had filled her body.

She let the earlier discussion of the final ritual of bonding fade away. Whatever the Completion was, she didn't have time for it, this morning anyway. If she were lucky, she would have time to snag a cup of coffee and a bit of breakfast before beginning the day. And a nap was already looking good.

"Okay. Shower." She rose quickly from the bed, watching as Alyx's cock began to stiffen. "And you keep that *thing* harnessed, dammit. It's dangerous."

Alyx looked down at his cock, then up at her. The smile he gave her was purely wicked. "Oh but, baby, he really likes you. Maybe just a friendly little pet before you go to work."

Lynn groaned as he placed his hand at the small of her back and led her to the bathroom. She could likely forget breakfast and coffee. But hell, it would be more than worth it.

Chapter Seventeen

🔊

Black really wasn't her color, Lynn thought later that day as she sat in the small sofa reading while Ariel St. James slept peacefully in the bed behind her. The other woman had seemed stronger today, doing more for herself than in the weeks previously.

Dark bruises still marred her skin, though. The dark, healing stripes of whiplashes covered her body. Thankfully, she hadn't been raped, though it had surprised Lynn that Ariel had escaped that final horror. Jonar wasn't known for his mercy.

Zach had assured her they were only days away from the arrival of Devlin's men, one of which claimed Ariel as his woman. Lynn had talked to Shanar several times by phone, and each time she was struck anew by the concern and harsh pain that filled the man's voice.

"Keep her safe, Miss Carstairs," he had whispered during the last conversation. "I will owe you more than my own life in exchange."

Lynn still wasn't clear why the Shadow warriors weren't guarding her themselves. It made little sense to her, that they had hired her brother's company rather than protecting Ariel personally.

"Lynn." The other woman's voice was faint, but appeared much stronger now.

Lynn rose to her feet, moving around the couch and approaching the bed.

"You should be resting." Lynn watched her carefully. Her color was good, her violet eyes not as dull or pain-filled as she had seen them at other times.

"I think I'm tired of sleeping." Ariel shifted on the bed, a bit of mocking humor filling her eyes. "I've done nothing but sleep for years, it seems."

"You were weak. Hurt." Lynn lowered herself to the chair beside the bed. "It takes a while to recover."

Ariel frowned. "I had some very weird dreams." She sighed. "Nightmares. At least, I hope they were nightmares."

They weren't nightmares, but Lynn wasn't about to tell her that. She didn't need the other woman worrying more than she obviously was.

"Would you like anything? Something to drink?" Lynn could see the weariness pulling at her again. Could *feel* the other woman fighting the drowsiness.

She could sense things she never had before. Ariel's increased energy, her irritation at her weakness, her incredible will to survive. Without it, she would have been dead long before her rescue from Jonar's fortress, let alone the pneumonia and internal injuries she had come out of there with.

Strangely enough, Lynn could also feel the healing of the other woman's body. Bones mending, muscles gaining strength, antibodies working to control and repair the damage. It was incredible, but draining.

"I'm fine." Ariel sighed deeply, her eyes fluttering once again. "Has there been a stranger here, Lynn?" she suddenly asked, her voice slurred with weariness. "A big guy. Really big. With stormy eyes and dark blond hair."

It sounded like Shanar Steele. "We have some big guys here." Lynn smiled as she thought of Alyx. "But none like that."

"Strange," Ariel muttered. "It's so strange what your mind dreams up."

She slipped back into sleep while Lynn watched her, confusion creasing her brow.

"Her warrior is tied to her. Through her soul and her crystal. He can come to her when she needs him to."

She turned to meet Alyx's somber gaze as he watched the other woman.

"You seem to know a lot about them." She rose to her feet, tucking the blankets carefully around Ariel's shoulders, making certain she was comfortable.

"You would remember as well, if you allowed yourself." He shrugged, his gaze still pensive, still resting on Ariel. "She was a warrioress, unlike any you could have known. Fierce. Strong. Her power flowed through her blade even though she denied its existence." He shook his head wearily. "Her death and the deaths of those who fought with her were mourned for centuries."

Reincarnation. Lynn shook her head. She had fought the acceptance of its existence for years. Even though her brothers debated it heavily, suspected their own lives were a result of past deeds unaccomplished. Still, she had fought it. Even though her own nightmares had increased, her sense of familiarity with the heiress she protected was so strong that she could almost anticipate her needs before she ever requested anything.

"All of this is very hard to accept," she said softly as she moved away from the bed and headed for the small sitting room.

As she passed Alyx, she felt his body heat enveloping her, calming her. She hadn't really noticed it before, how so much of him leaned toward her, wrapping around her protectively whenever he was near. And she flowed toward him as well. It was disconcerting, *feeling* herself leaning into him, her energy flowing toward him.

She had known she was drawn to him before, that resisting him was next to impossible, but feeling everything inside her reinforcing that connection sent shivers up her spine.

"It will become easier," he promised her as he followed her into the room, stepping closer to her, his hand trailing up her spine. "You need to relax. To allow the changes a chance to settle within you."

There were too many at times. She could feel an influx of power at the oddest moments, knowledge she had never had before, a control over not just the former powers, but also the additional ones, that she never could have hoped to attain before meeting Alyx.

"So all it takes is fucking you to gain the power?" She winced as the words escaped her lips. Dammit. She hadn't meant it that way. But perhaps she had. She had been fine before that morning in his room. Before she had allowed his climax to spill into her mouth.

He chuckled. "That would make it so much easier to accept, would it not, beloved?"

She flashed him an irritated glance. "Yeah. It would."

He shook his head at her chidingly. "You know better."

Yeah. She did. Something else had happened to her that morning, something she didn't want to look into too deeply. A part of her had unlocked, opening up for him. An emotion, a commitment to him that she had never given to another living soul. She had a terribly bad feeling she had fallen in love with Alyx, Dragon Prime, long before that.

"I need to know what happens next." She couldn't put it off any longer.

Silence met her demand. Lynn turned back to him, staring up at him, once again amazed by the shifting color in his eyes. They were like living mercury, ebbing and flowing in response to whatever emotions filled him at the time.

He watched her closely, his expression staying calm, almost serene.

"Next, is the Completion." He finally shrugged. "The knowledge and acceptance of all that will change within you is like an unopened box buried deep in your soul. Before Completion can be attained you must look into it, let it flow through you and know that is what you want. Above all things, you must want it."

Lynn pressed her lips tightly together. There may never be a Completion then. She saw that knowledge in Alyx's eyes, the sadness that shifted through the swirling silver color. He knew, as well as she did, how much she regretted the gifts she carried.

"Ahh, gentle heart." He touched her cheek, his expression tightening as remorse fill the air around them, so thick it pierced her soul. "Think, my beloved Lynn. Remember the lives saved. The joy you've brought. Think of all you could lose. All that would have never been, had you not been so blessed. Would it really be worth throwing away?"

She looked away from him. She couldn't stare into his eyes, couldn't bear his pain. He had lived so long, waited for her, needed her, and she would willingly throw it away for the peace of blissful ignorance. Wouldn't she?

"No, Lynn." His voice was gentle and so filled with regret it broke her heart. "You wouldn't change it. Though you may well die believing otherwise."

Lynn flinched as he turned and stalked away from her. She could feel the sparks of fury lashing out at her, deflected by the clothing, but there all the same.

"It's my life." She fought to breathe, to convince herself she was right. To convince herself it should have been her choice.

"Sadly, it is at that." The door slammed closed behind him as she stood there, alone. Empty. And wondering if even she knew what she really wanted.

Chapter Eighteen

ை

Would she have changed it? Darkness was rolling in
now, the sun setting slowly over the mountains as Lynn lay
in her bed, still dressed in the black clothes, debating with
herself over the matter. She didn't like the answers she was
coming to.

She would have, she assured herself. Ignorance was
bliss. Right? *Wrong!* Something inside her sneered
mockingly.

She closed her eyes, determined to still the riotous
emotions building inside her. What did it matter? She
couldn't change it. She was stuck with it. Didn't she make
the most of it?

Behind her closed eyelids a scene slowly took shape.
Her heart beat in dread, fear rolling over her. A battlefield.
Ariel lay, dressed in leather, feet away from her, bloodied
and dead. Other women and several men lay similarly. All
lifeless.

The battle had cost them their lives. It had cost Lynn
her soul.

If only, Alyx, I had known... She felt the words whisper
through her mind. Impressions and thoughts that she
shouldn't have known, shouldn't have experienced, drifting
through her mind. Nightmares she had refused to delve
into, until now, suddenly crystal clear.

She hated the sudden flashes of memory that had no
place in the time she lived within. She had always cursed
them. Always regretted them. Until now. Now, when she

could look at them and know what she had thrown away so long ago. She could have been within Alyx's arms all these years. Awaiting the time when Ariel needed her again. Perhaps being there to stop the attack Jonar had made on her.

Her chest tightened at her own foolishness. For so many years she had fought the very strength and energy that made her who and what she was. She had fought the dreams that tried to warn her and her own deeply buried wishes. She had wanted Alyx to find her. Had needed him to open the door to her own fears, her own knowledge of who she was. Without him, she would always be missing a part of her soul. Because he was a part of it.

And she had hurt him. She hadn't meant to. She had, once again, given into her own fears. It seemed that risking her life wasn't as hard for her as risking her heart had become.

The heart breaks easier. And the body goes on; living when the heart withers away in the chest, creating a wound that never heals.

Lynn jerked in surprise as Alyx's voice whispered through her mind.

She blinked. She could *feel* him. Not in the sense that she was reading his mind, but she could actually feel his soul, his inner being reaching out to her.

You could do the same, he whispered through her head. *All you have to do is open that part of you, Lynn. Allow it freedom. Release the one thing you are most terrified of.*

She flinched. He needed the Completion. Whatever the hell that was. But did she know how to give him what she knew they both needed?

He was silent now. Waiting. She could feel him inside her, like a warm, comforting shadow. Patient. Encouraging her to give in to the nightmares that taunted her for years.

She had spent so long hiding, how was she supposed to learn to embrace it overnight?

I don't know how. She felt lost. Alone inside despite the knowledge he was there. She could feel the incompleteness of whatever bond it was they shared.

You know, Lynn. It's there inside you. A part of you. You only have to find it.

Lynn stared up at the ceiling, frowning. The part of her that most terrified her. Her powers. Losing complete control of the shifting, ever-changing energy that built inside her like a monster ready to devour anything and everything in its path. If the secrets resided there, she might never find them.

Control is merely an illusion, beloved. His whisper seemed to pulse around her. *You know this as well as I. The powers are what they are. Nothing more. Nothing less. They are for you to use, however you see fit to use them. They neither control nor are controlled. They simply exist.*

She moved from the bed. Nothing was going to get accomplished this way. Nothing was going to be decided. She could stare at the ceiling all night long and it would never reveal the answers she needed. If she was going to be tormented with questions and the lack of answers, then by God, Alyx would share in the agony. Or the pleasure. Whichever came first.

* * * * *

Alyx waited for her. His body was tense, his lust like a demon riding him. But she had to make the next move. She had to come to him. She had to complete the cycle of power and release the Dar-phantom from its confinement within the Dragon stone. It would complete the bond. It would seal them together forever. That energy, a part of her, a part of him, binding them together.

135

He could feel the Dragon stone heating at his breast as she came nearer to his room. He forced himself to wait. To lie still. His cock was stone hard, throbbing in anticipation. She was unaware of it, but he could feel it. The Completion was on her. Her greatest fear, the fear of losing her heart, her soul to another, was slowly easing.

She didn't have to acknowledge it in words. As long as her inner being knew the truth, then the rest of her would follow. And he could feel her inner being reaching out to him, drawn to his own and the power they were destined to share.

The door opened and there she stood. Framed within the light of the hallway, her hair a dark halo around her exquisite face, her lean, graceful body defined by the skin cloth. Cloth that had seared his soul in the making. Infused with his love for her. His strength. His need. Sewn together with painfully extracted bits of his own power. Power fused from the metaphysical to the physical. Given cohesion and balance. She wore on her body a part of his being.

The door closed behind her and before his admiring eyes the cloth peeled away from her body and floated to the floor by the simple means of her own thoughts.

Her eyes were narrowed. Intense. She was there to still both their demons and she would do so with a power that even she could not realize.

"If you come to this bed, you begin the Completion," he warned her softly as she neared him. "Know that, Lynn. What your mind has not yet accepted, your soul has."

Her lips lifted, a rather endearing turn of resignation. "My soul accepts nothing that my mind doesn't first approve." Her voice was like shimmering threads of lust and emotion. "Perhaps you should remember that, Alyx."

"You will not have the control I see you are determined to keep," he told her gently. "There will be no stopping, Lynn. No going back. Know that before you come to me."

She braced her hands on the foot of the bed, moving slowly forward, crawling between his splayed thighs on hands and knees like a slender cat, her eyes narrowed, hunger glittering in the depths.

The Dragon stone pulsed. His cock throbbed. His body tightened nearly to the breaking point as he felt a warm puff of air, directed from her pouted lips to the drawn sac at the base of his erection.

He would wait. There was little sense in taking this measure of her control before the time demanded it. He could feel the Dar-phantom strengthening, swirling within the stone as the dragon flexed against his flesh.

When her tongue, so small, moist and filled with heat, swiped a path of erotic destruction along the tightened flesh, he couldn't halt the groan that tore from his throat.

There she was, on hands and knees, her head lowered, her eyes watching him as she began to torture the already strained baggage. She sipped at the taut skin, licked it, scraped it gently with her teeth and all the while her eyes glittered with the power growing inside her.

Sexual, primal heat filled the room. Alyx kept himself still only by a strength of will he was unaware he possessed. He wanted to jerk her to him, throw her to the bed and pound into her until she screamed in orgasm. But now was not the time. The Completion demanded so much more.

Her tongue licked him delicately as it moved from his scrotum, up along the base of his cock, then painted the shaft with a trail of sensual heat that had him gripping the blankets with white-knuckled strength. She suckled at the heavy ridged veins, licked over them with a hum of appreciation, then moved to the wide, bulging head.

"Mercy." He wasn't above pleading in this instance.

Her mouth surrounded the throbbing head, suckling lightly then tonguing the crest beneath in a way that sent flares of electricity shooting from his cock, up his spine and into the base of his skull.

The pre-seminal fluid began to ease from the dual tips, only to be licked away by a capricious, mischievous tongue intent on driving him insane. Then once again she sucked him into her mouth, hollowing her cheeks, creating a flashpoint of sensation as her mouth moved up and down with shallow thrusts that had him gritting his teeth against the need to orgasm.

And still, her eyes glowed. A deep, vibrant hazel that slowly built, intensifying as she loosened the extreme self-control she had always held over her powers.

He knew the moment she realized what was happening to her. Her mouth stilled, her eyes widened, and then he struck. He would not allow her the time to adjust to the build-up. To do so would cause her mind to shut down, her fears to close off the avenue of escape he had been building just for this moment.

Chapter Nineteen

❧

Before Lynn could adjust to the strange sensations suddenly building beneath her skin, Alyx had gripped her shoulders, pulling her along his body before flipping her on her back to the bed.

She moved to escape him. To attempt to slide across the bed and away from him, but as always, he was a staggering step ahead of her. He kneed her thighs apart, sliding down her body, his shoulders wedging between them as his lips pressed to the slick, drenched flesh of her pussy.

Lynn nearly went through the ceiling. It was unlike anything he had done to her before. A kiss that shattered any control, that swept over her like a hurricane destroying any thoughts in its path. His tongue sank into her vagina, thrusting with hot, deep penetrations that had her lifting to him; desperate mewls for more escaping her lips.

The more her cream flowed from her body, the harder he lapped at it, eating her with such primal male satisfaction she lost all control. She could feel the power building inside her, heating her from the inside out, driving her closer and closer to a brink that should have terrified her. Should have. But she knew Alyx would catch her. Knew he would be there to keep her from harm.

Tighter and tighter the coil of passion-hot flames tightened in her belly, seared her pussy. Her body tingled, heated further until it felt as though fire licked over her flesh. Her nerve endings were electrified, breasts swollen, nipples peaked like hard little diamond points begging for attention.

"Alyx," she gasped as she felt the explosion nearing.

In response, his fingers slid through the juices of her pussy, moved lower, one strong, broad finger penetrating, impaling the tender opening to her anus.

Rockets went off inside her as her orgasm consumed her. It was like the Fourth of July times ten, setting off sharp, sudden detonations within her pussy that had her juices flooding it, pouring to his mouth to be consumed by his greedy lips.

A growl shattered the room as he came to his knees, his finger sliding free of her ass, his arms extending. Lynn could only watch in shock. The Dragon stone at his chest glowed brightly, then a strange, illuminating white fog began to pour free.

Lynn was within a second of being terrified back into an unresponsive state. But at the same time, Alyx's hips moved, burying his jutting cock deep inside her pussy with a thrust that seared every nerve ending it could have possessed.

The heavy ridges and erect cock's crest stroked through her tight channel, separating her, stretching her as her eyes closed and she arched closer, deepening the thrust.

She didn't want to see what the mist was doing. Didn't want to know... Her eyes flew open.

"Oh. My. God. Alyx!" Her strangled scream tore from her throat as a form of pure white light settled over her body.

Hands plumped her breasts, the feel of a warm, heated mouth covered each tip. Alyx was buried deep and hard inside her, his head thrown back in ecstasy as a similar light flowed over him, around him, as it began to creep toward her.

She shuddered as his cock began to move. Slow, deep thrusts as a tentative heat began to work down the cleft of her buttocks. Shock should have been holding her rigid; instead, pleasure began to fill her, stroking beneath her skin, caressing her in ways that pushed her ever higher. She was a creature of sensuality now. Accepting each caress, glorying in it.

Heat moved lower between the cheeks of her rear, stroking her gently, then probing at the small entrance to her ass. Her legs were lifted. Alyx's hands guided them until her feet rested on his shoulders, his silver eyes glowing as he stared down at her.

"Knowledge of the power..." He pulled his cock back then pushed deep and hard as the heat behind her impaled her anus.

"Alyx. Please. I can't stand it." She was shaking with pleasure; with an intensity that she feared would destroy her.

"Acceptance of the bond." His cock pulled free as the energy filled her. Stretching her. First her pussy as it gushed its juices, then her anus, widening the entrance with a streak of pleasure/pain that had her gasping.

Alyx gripped the shaft of his cock, rubbing it against the slowly opening portal.

"Completion, Lynn," he whispered. "A part of me, forever a part of you."

He surged inside her anus. The muscles parted like soft butter, lubricated by the energy filling her and the pre-seminal fluid coating his cock. She was impaled. Stretched in ways she could have never imagined as her cunt caught fire from the feel of another cock, one of pure, white-hot energy filling it.

Alyx gripped her thighs, his face twisting into lines of sublime pleasure as he began to fuck her with deep powerful strokes into her bottom. The energy filling her fucked in a steady, hard rhythm into her pussy. Destroying her.

The coil of electricity fused inside her womb, growing, tightening, piercing her with sensations she feared she would never survive. Then she exploded.

Alyx's cock began to ripple inside her anus, the cock's crest stroking, flexing, as the heavy ridges rasped her sensitive tissue. She tightened on him, her back bowing, driving him deeper, harder inside her as she felt every cell in her body unravel. Felt them open and felt the power of the whitened form flowing into her.

It was never ending. It was death and rebirth and her scream echoed around them as she felt the hard, powerful pulse of his climax searing her anus, flowing deep and hard inside her, burning her with a pleasure she knew she would be begging to experience again.

"I love you!" She screamed the words as her soul opened, her heart exploding with the power of the emotion she fought, and failed, to contain within her. "God help me, Alyx, I love you."

And she was complete.

Alyx collapsed over her, his rough voice whispering his love for her. His hands were gentle, soothing her as his cock began to slip free of the tight grip she had held on it.

Sweat coated them, dripped from their bodies, dampening the sheets beneath them. The air was thick with satiation and an emotion that made tears come to her eyes. Love. Love in a form so rich, so intense, it was indeed physical.

"Always now," Alyx whispered at her ear. "Always, Lynn. Always mine."

Epilogue

&

Gryphon felt the force vibrate within his Gryphon stone. A Prime Warrior had finished the Completion and brought his bond mate to the other side. It was a time that would be rejoiced for days by Prime and Initiate Warriors alike. It created another bonded pair, which would in turn create children with the power to strike fast and hard at the darkness overtaking their land.

It was the first bonding in a thousand years. He could hear the Dragon Master bellowing his pride to the Gryphon and Phoenix who shared his quest. And he knew that either himself or the Phoenix Prime would be next. Their bond mates were here, on this planet, as had been foretold so many millennia ago.

His thoughts turned then to a female warrior. His eyes narrowed. She was his. He had known it long ago, but had hesitated in making his claim. She would not be easy to conquer. The Completion was something she would fight. But she would accept it. Eventually.

He would be next. He felt his Gryphon stone heat at his chest as the Dar-phantom sighed in agreement. Yes. He would take his bond mate soon. Whether she wished it or not.

Why an electronic book?

We live in the Information Age—an exciting time in the history of human civilization, in which technology rules supreme and continues to progress in leaps and bounds every minute of every day. For a multitude of reasons, more and more avid literary fans are opting to purchase e-books instead of paper books. The question from those not yet initiated into the world of electronic reading is simply: *Why?*

1. *Price.* An electronic title at Ellora's Cave Publishing and Cerridwen Press runs anywhere from 40% to 75% less than the cover price of the exact same title in paperback format. Why? Basic mathematics and cost. It is less expensive to publish an e-book (no paper and printing, no warehousing and shipping) than it is to publish a paperback, so the savings are passed along to the consumer.

2. *Space.* Running out of room in your house for your books? That is one worry you will never have with electronic books. For a low one-time cost, you can purchase a handheld device specifically designed for e-reading. Many e-readers have large, convenient screens for viewing. Better yet, hundreds of titles can be stored within your new library—on a single microchip. There are a variety of e-readers from different manufacturers. You can also read e-books on your PC or laptop computer. (Please note that Ellora's Cave does not endorse any specific brands.

You can check our websites at www.ellorascave.com or www.cerridwenpress.com for information we make available to new consumers.)

3. *Mobility.* Because your new e-library consists of only a microchip within a small, easily transportable e-reader, your entire cache of books can be taken with you wherever you go.

4. *Personal Viewing Preferences.* Are the words you are currently reading too small? Too large? Too... ANNOYING? Paperback books cannot be modified according to personal preferences, but e-books can.

5. *Instant Gratification.* Is it the middle of the night and all the bookstores near you are closed? Are you tired of waiting days, sometimes weeks, for bookstores to ship the novels you bought? Ellora's Cave Publishing sells instantaneous downloads twenty-four hours a day, seven days a week, every day of the year. Our webstore is never closed. Our e-book delivery system is 100% automated, meaning your order is filled as soon as you pay for it.

Those are a few of the top reasons why electronic books are replacing paperbacks for many avid readers.

As always, Ellora's Cave and Cerridwen Press welcome your questions and comments. We invite you to email us at Comments@ellorascave.com or write to us directly at Ellora's Cave Publishing Inc., 1056 Home Avenue, Akron, OH 44310-3502.

erridwen, the Celtic Goddess of wisdom, was the muse who brought inspiration to storytellers and those in the creative arts. Cerridwen Press encompasses the best and most innovative stories in all genres of today's fiction. Visit our site and discover the newest titles by talented authors who still get inspired - much like the ancient storytellers did, once upon a time.

Cerridwen Press

www.cerridwenpress.com

*Discover for yourself why readers can't get enough
of the multiple award-winning publisher*

Ellora's Cave.

Whether you prefer e-books or paperbacks,

be sure to visit EC on the web at
www.ellorascave.com

*for an erotic reading experience that will leave you
breathless.*